O9-AID-184

"Her stories have fueled the dreams of twenty-five million readers."
—*Entertainment Weekly*

* * *

"All right," Rowan snapped, "I admit I was attracted to you. But you were the one who kissed me."

"I did indeed," Liam murmured. He wanted to do so again right now.

"And I overreacted." The memory still made her blood heat. "You had a perfect right to tell me to go, but you didn't have to be so unkind about it. Obviously, you didn't have the same...response I did."

"I kissed you because I wanted to. My response to you was more...acute than I'd bargained for. So I was unkind. I'll apologize for that, Rowan, but only for that."

"You're sorry for being unkind, or for having a response to me?"

"For both, if it comes to it."

Dear Reader,

What is there to say about a month with a new Nora Roberts title except "Hurry up and get to the store!" *Enchanted* is a mysterious, romantic and utterly irresistible follow-up to THE DONOVAN LEGACY trilogy, which appeared several years ago and is currently being reissued. It's the kind of story only Nora can tell—and boy, will you be glad she did!

The rest of our month is pretty special, too, so pick up a few more books to keep you warm. Try *The Admiral's Bride,* by Suzanne Brockmann, the latest TALL, DARK & DANGEROUS title. These navy SEAL heroes are fast staking claim to readers' hearts all over the world. Read about the last of THE SISTERS WASKOWITZ in Kathleen Creighton's *Eve's Wedding Knight.* You'll love it—and you'll join me in hoping we revisit these fascinating women—and their irresistible heroes—someday. *Rio Grande Wedding* is the latest from multiaward-winning Ruth Wind, a part of her MEN OF THE LAND miniseries, featuring the kind of Southwestern men no self-respecting heroine can resist. Take a look at Vickie Taylor's *Virgin Without a Memory,* a book *you'll* remember for a long time. And finally, welcome Harlequin Historical author Mary McBride to the contemporary romance lineup. *Just One Look* will demand more than just one look from you, and it will have you counting the days until she sets another story in the present day.

And, of course, mark your calendar and come back next month, when Silhouette Intimate Moments will once again bring you six of the most excitingly romantic novels you'll ever find.

Enjoy!

Leslie J. Wainger
Executive Senior Editor

Please address questions and book requests to:
Silhouette Reader Service
U.S.: 3010 Walden Ave., P.O. Box 1325, Buffalo, NY 14269
Canadian: P.O. Box 609, Fort Erie, Ont. L2A 5X3

NORA ROBERTS

Enchanted

THE DONOVAN LEGACY

Silhouette®
INTIMATE™MOMENTS®

Published by Silhouette Books

America's Publisher of Contemporary Romance

If you purchased this book without a cover you should be aware
that this book is stolen property. It was reported as "unsold and
destroyed" to the publisher, and neither the author nor the
publisher has received any payment for this "stripped book."

To the friends I've made in cyberspace,
with gratitude for the hours of fun

 SILHOUETTE BOOKS

ISBN 0-373-07961-3

ENCHANTED

Copyright © 1999 by Nora Roberts

All rights reserved. Except for use in any review, the reproduction
or utilization of this work in whole or in part in any form by any
electronic, mechanical or other means, now known or hereafter
invented, including xerography, photocopying and recording, or in
any information storage or retrieval system, is forbidden without
the written permission of the editorial office, Silhouette Books,
300 East 42nd Street, New York, NY 10017 U.S.A.

All characters in this book have no existence outside the imagination of
the author and have no relation whatsoever to anyone bearing the same
name or names. They are not even distantly inspired by any individual
known or unknown to the author, and all incidents are pure invention.

This edition published by arrangement with Harlequin Books S.A.

® and TM are trademarks of Harlequin Books S.A., used under license.
Trademarks indicated with ® are registered in the United States Patent
and Trademark Office, the Canadian Trade Marks Office and in other
countries.

Look us up on-line at: http://www.romance.net

Printed in U.S.A.

NORA ROBERTS

is a publishing phenomenon, not only getting eleven of her titles on the *New York Times* bestseller list in a single year, but also hitting the #1 spot. She has written over a hundred novels, more than eighty of them for Silhouette Books, and has over fifty million books in print. Her work has been optioned and made into films, excerpted in *Good Housekeeping* and has been translated into over twenty-five languages and published all over the world.

Whether writing romance, mystery or mainstream novels, Nora Roberts is a consummate storyteller who has enchanted and delighted millions with her captivating stories—and keeps her readers coming back for more.

THE DONOVANS

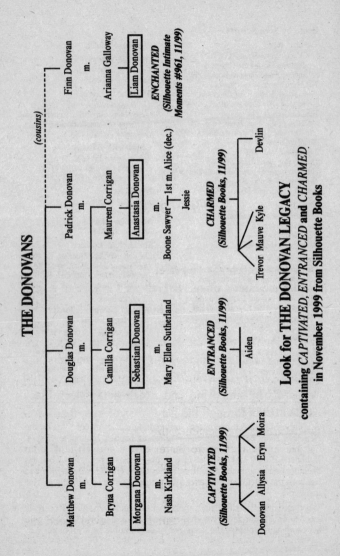

(cousins)

Matthew Donovan
m.
Bryna Corrigan

Douglas Donovan
m.
Camilla Corrigan

Padrick Donovan
m.
Maureen Corrigan

Finn Donovan
m.
Arianna Galloway

Morgana Donovan
m.
Nash Kirkland

Sebastian Donovan
m.
Mary Ellen Sutherland

Anastasia Donovan
m.
Boone Sawyer ⊤ 1st m. Alice (dec.)
Jessie

Liam Donovan

ENCHANTED
(Silhouette Intimate
Moments #961, 11/99)

CAPTIVATED
(Silhouette Books, 11/99)

Donovan Allysia Eryn Moira

ENTRANCED
(Silhouette Books, 11/99)

Aiden

CHARMED
(Silhouette Books, 11/99)

Trevor Mauve Kyle

Devlin

Look for THE DONOVAN LEGACY
containing *CAPTIVATED*, *ENTRANCED* and *CHARMED*
in November 1999 from Silhouette Books

Prologue

Dark as the night and fleet of foot, the wolf raced under a hunter's moon. He ran for the love of it, and he ran alone, through the grand tower of trees, the purple shadows of the forest, the magic of the night.

The wind from across the sea spewed across the pines, sent them singing songs of the ancients and spilling their scent into the air. Small creatures with eyes that gleamed hid and watched the sleek black shape bullet through the lacy layer of mist that shimmered down the beaten path.

He knew they were there, could smell them, hear the rapid beat of their blood. But he hunted nothing that night but the night itself.

He had no pack, no mate but solitude.

A restlessness lived in him that not even speed and freedom could quell. In his quest for peace, he haunted the forest, stalked the cliffs, circled the clearings, but nothing soothed or satisfied.

As the path rose more steeply and the trees began to thin, he slowed to a trot, scenting the air. There was…something in the air, something that had lured him out to the cliffs high above the restless Pacific. With powerful strides he climbed the rocks, his golden eyes scanning, seeking.

There, at the topmost point where the waves crashed like cannon fire and the moon swam white and full, he raised his head and called. To sea, to sky, to night.

To magic.

The howl echoed, spread, filled the night with both demand and question. With power as natural as breath.

And the whispers that flickered back told him only that a change was coming. Endings, beginnings. Destiny.

His fate was waiting for him.

Again the rogue black wolf with gold eyes threw back his head and called. There was more, and he would have it. Now the earth shook, and the water swirled. Far over the sea a single spear of lightning broke the blackness with a blinding white flash. In its afterglow for an instant—a heartbeat only—was the answer.

Love waits.

And the magic trembled on the air, danced over the sea with a sound that might have been laughter. Tiny sparks of light skimmed over the surface, bobbing, twirling to spin into the star-strewn sky in a gilt cloud.

The wolf watched, and he listened. Even when he turned back to the forest and its shadows, the answer trailed after him.

Love waits.

As the restlessness in him grew, beat with his heart, he shot down the path, powerful strides tearing the fog to ribbons. Now his blood heated with the speed, and veering left, he broke through the trees toward the soft glow of lights. There the cabin stood sturdy, its windows shining with welcome. The whispers of the night fell quiet.

As he bounded up the steps, white smoke swirled, blue light shimmered. And wolf became man.

Chapter 1

When Rowan Murray got her first look at the cabin, she was filled with a sense of both relief and fear. Relief that she'd finally come to the end of the long drive from San Francisco to this sheltered spot on the coast of Oregon. And fear for the exact same reason.

She was here. She had done it.

What next?

The practical thing, of course, was to get out of the four-wheel drive, unlock the front door and give herself a tour of the place she intended to make home for the next three months. Unpack what belongings she'd brought with her. Make herself some tea. Take a hot shower.

Yes, those were all practical, reasonable things to do, she told herself. And she sat exactly where she was, in the driver's seat of the two-week-old Range

Rover, her long, slender fingers gripping white-knuckled on the wheel.

She was alone. Completely, absolutely alone.

It was what she wanted, what she needed. What she'd pushed herself to accomplish for months so that when the offer of the cabin had come, she'd snatched it as if it were a tree limb and she'd been sinking in quicksand.

Now that she had it, she couldn't even get out of the car.

"You're such a fool, Rowan." She whispered it, leaning back, closing her eyes for just a moment. "Such a coward."

She sat, gathering her energies, a small, slenderly built woman with creamy skin that had lost its sheen of rose. Her hair was straight as rain and the color of polished oak. Now, she wore it pulled back, out of the way, in a thick braid that was coming loose. Her nose was long and sharp, her mouth just slightly over wide for the triangle of her face. Her eyes, tired now from hours of driving, were a deep, dark blue, long lidded and tilted at the corners.

Elf's eyes, her father often said. And thinking of that, she felt tears welling up in them.

She'd disappointed him, and her mother. The guilt of that weighed like a stone on her heart. She hadn't been able to explain, not clearly enough, not well enough, why she'd hadn't been capable of continuing on the path they'd so carefully cleared for her. Every step she'd taken on it had been a strain, as if every step had taken her farther and farther away from where she needed to be.

What she needed to be.

So in the end she'd run. Oh, not in actuality. She was much too reasonable to have run away like a thief in the night. She'd made specific plans, followed concrete steps, but under it all she'd been fleeing from home, from career, from family. From the love that was smothering her as surely as if its hands had been clamped over her nose and mouth.

Here, she'd promised herself, she'd be able to breathe, to think, to decide. And maybe, just maybe, to understand what it was that kept her from being what everyone seemed to want her to be.

If in the end, she discovered she was wrong and everyone else was right, she was prepared to deal with it. But she would take these three months for herself.

She opened her eyes again, let herself look. And as she did, her muscles slowly relaxed. It was so beautiful, she realized. The grand majesty of trees shooting up into the sky and whistling in the wind, the two-story cabin tucked into a private glen, the silver flash of sun off the busy little steam that snaked to the west.

The cabin itself gleamed dark gold in the sunlight. Its wood was smooth, its windows sparkled. The little covered porch looked perfect for sitting on lazy mornings or quiet evenings. From where she sat, she thought she could see the brave spears of spring bulbs testing the air.

They'd find it chilly yet, she mused. Belinda had warned her to buy flannel, and to expect spring to come late to this little corner of the world.

Well, she knew how to build a fire, she told herself,

glancing at the stone chimney. One of her favorite spots in her parents' house had been in the big sprawling living room beside the hearth with a fire crackling against the damp chill of the city.

She'd build one as soon as she was settled, she promised herself. To welcome herself to her new home.

Steadier, she opened the door, stepped out. Her heavy boots snapped a thick twig with a sound like a bullet. She pressed a hand to her heart, laughing a little. New boots for the city girl, she thought. Jingling the keys just to make noise, she walked to the cabin, up the two steps to the porch. She slipped the key she'd labeled *front door* into the lock and, taking a slow breath, pushed the door open.

And fell in love.

"Oh, would you look at this!" A smile lit her face as she stepped inside, circled. "Belinda, God bless you."

The walls were the color of warmly toasted bread, framed in dark wood, accented with the magical paintings her friend was renowned for. The hearth was stone, scrubbed clean and laid with kindling and logs in welcome. Colorful rugs were scattered over the polished wood floor. The furnishings were simple, clean lines, with deep cushions that picked up those wonderful tones of emerald, sapphire and ruby.

To complete the fairy-tale aspect, there were statues of dragons, wizards, bowls filled with stones or dried flowers, and sparkling geodes. Charmed, Rowan dashed up the stairs and hugged herself as she toured the two large rooms there.

One, full of light from a ring of windows, was obviously her friend's studio when she used the cabin. Canvases, paints and brushes were neatly stored, an easel stood empty, a smock hung, paint-splattered, on a brass hook.

Even here there were pretty touches—fat white candles in silver holders, glass stars, a globe of smoky crystal.

The bedroom thrilled her with its huge canopy bed draped in white linen, the little fireplace to warm the room, the carved rosewood armoire.

It felt…peaceful, Rowan realized. Settled, content, welcoming. Yes, she could breathe here. She could think here. For some inexplicable reason, she felt she could belong here.

Anxious now to begin settling in, she hurried downstairs, out the door she'd left open to her SUV. She'd grabbed the first box from the cargo area, when the skin on the back of her neck prickled. Suddenly her heart thundered in her chest, and her palms sprang with damp.

She turned quickly, managed only one strangled gasp.

The wolf was pure black with eyes like gold coins. And it stood at the edge of the trees, still as a statue carved from onyx. Watching her. She could do no more than stare while her pulse beat like fury. Why wasn't she screaming? she asked herself. Why wasn't she running?

Why was she more surprised than afraid?

Had she dreamed of him? Couldn't she just catch the edge of some misty dream where he'd run through the mist toward her? Is that why he seemed so familiar, almost...expected?

But that was ridiculous. She'd never seen a wolf outside of a zoo in her life. Surely she'd never seen one who stared so patiently at her. Into her.

"Hello." She heard herself speak with a kind of dull shock, and followed it with a nervous laugh. Then she blinked, and he was gone.

For a moment, she swayed, like a woman coming out of a trance. When she shook herself clear, she stared at the edge of the trees, searching for some movement, some shadow, some sign.

But there was only silence.

"Imagining things again," she muttered, shifting the box, turning away. "If there was anything there, it was a dog. Just a dog."

Wolves were nocturnal, weren't they? They didn't approach people in broad daylight, just stand and stare, then vanish.

She'd look it up to be sure, but it had been a dog. She was positive now. Belinda hadn't mentioned anything about neighbors or other cabins. And how odd, Rowan thought now, that she hadn't even asked about it.

Well, there was a neighbor somewhere, and he had a big, beautiful, black dog. She imagined they could all keep out of each others' way.

The wolf watched from the shadows of the trees. Who was the woman? he wondered. *Why* was the woman? She moved quickly, a little nervously, tossing glances over her shoulder as she carried things from the car to the cabin.

He'd scented her from half a mile away. Her fears, her excitement, her longings had all come to him. And had brought him to her.

His eyes narrowed with annoyance. His teeth bared in challenge. He'd be damned if he'd take her. Damned if he let her change what he was or what he wanted.

Sleek and silent, he turned away and vanished into the thick trees.

Rowan built a fire, delighted when the logs crackled and caught. She unpacked systematically. There wasn't much, really. Clothes, supplies. Most of the boxes she'd hauled in were filled with books. Books she couldn't live without, books she'd promised herself she'd make time to read. Books to study, books for pleasure. She'd grown up with a love of reading, of exploring worlds through words. And because of that great love, she often questioned her own dissatisfaction with teaching.

It should have been the right goal, just as her parents always insisted. She embraced learning and had always learned well and quickly. She'd studied, took her major and then her master's in Education. At twenty-seven, she'd already taught full-time for nearly six years.

She was good at it, she thought now as she sipped tea while standing in front of the blazing fire. She could recognize the strengths and weaknesses of her students, home in on their interests and on how to challenge them.

Yet she dragged her feet on getting her doctorate. She woke each morning vaguely discontent and came home each evening unsatisfied.

Because her heart had never been in it.

When she'd tried to explain that to the people who loved her, they'd been baffled. Her students loved and respected her, the administration at her school valued her. Why wasn't she pursuing her degree, marrying Alan, completing her nice, tidy life as she should?

Why, indeed, she thought. Because the only answer she had for them, and for herself, was in her heart.

And brooding wasn't thinking, she reminded herself. She'd go for a walk, get a sense of where she was. She wanted to see the cliffs Belinda had told her of.

She locked the door out of habit, then drew in a deep gulp of air that tasted of pine and sea. In her mind she could see the quick sketch Belinda had drawn her of the cabin, the forest, the cliffs. Ignoring her nerves, she stepped onto the path and headed due west.

She'd never lived outside of the city. Growing up in San Francisco hadn't prepared her for the vastness of the Oregon forest, its smells, its sounds. Even so, her nerves began to fade into wonder.

It was like a book, a gorgeously rich story full of color and texture. The giant Douglas firs towered over her, their bushy branches letting the sun splatter into a shifting, luminous, gilded green light nearly the color of the moss that grew so thick and soft on the ground. The trees chilled the air with their shade, scented it with their fragrance.

The forest floor was soft with shed needles and ripe with the tang of sap.

At their bases, ferns grew thick and green, some thin and sharp as swords, others lacy as fans. Like faeries, she thought in a moment's fancy, who only danced at night.

The stream bubbled along, skimming over rocks worn round and smooth, tumbling down a little rise with a sudden rush of white water that looked impossibly pure and cold. She followed the wind of it, relaxed with its music.

There was a bend up ahead, she thought idly, and around the corner there would be a stump of an old tree on the left that looked like an old man's worn face. Foxglove grew there, and in the summer it would grow tall and pale purple. It was a good place to sit, that stump, and watch the forest come to life around you.

She stopped when she came to it, staring blankly at the gnarled bark that did indeed look like an old man's face. How had she known this would be here? she wondered, rubbing the heel of her hand on her suddenly speeding heart. It wasn't on Belinda's sketch, so how had she known?

"Because she mentioned it. She told me about it, that's all. It's just the sort of fanciful thing she'd tell me, and that I'd forget about."

But Rowan didn't sit, didn't wait for the forest to come to life. It already felt alive. Enchanted, she thought and managed to smile. The enchanted woods every girl dreams of where the faeries dance and the prince waits to rescue her from the jealous hag or the evil wizard.

There was nothing to fear here. The woods were hers as long as she wanted. There was no one to shake their heads indulgently if her mind wandered toward fairy tales and the foolish. Her dreams were her own as well.

If she had a dream, or a story to tell a young girl, Rowan decided, it would be about the enchanted forest...and the prince who wandered it, searching through the green light and greener shadow for his one true love. He was under a spell, she thought, and trapped in the sleek, handsome form of a black wolf. Until the maiden came and freed him with her courage, her wit, and with her love.

She sighed once, wishing she had a talent for the details of telling stories. She wasn't bad at themes, she mused, but she could never figure out how to turn a theme into an engaging tale.

So she read instead, and admired those who could.

She heard the sea, like an echo of memory, and turned unerringly onto the left fork of the path. What began as a whisper became a roar, and she started to hurry, was nearly running by the time she burst out of the trees and saw the cliffs.

Her boots clattered as she climbed up the rocks. The wind kicked and tore what was left of her braid loose so that her hair flew wild and free. Her laughter rang out, full of delight as she came breathlessly to the top of the rise.

It was, without a doubt, the most magnificent sight

she'd ever seen. Miles of blue ocean, hemmed with fuming white waves that threw themselves in fury against the rocks below. The afternoon sun showered over it, sprinkling jewels onto that undulating mat of blue.

She could see boats in the distance, riding the waves, and a small forested island rising out of the sea like a bunched fist.

Gleaming black mussels clung to the rocks below her, and as she looked closer, she saw the thorny brown sticks of a bird's nest tucked into a crevice. On impulse she got down, bellied out and was rewarded by a glimpse of eggs.

Pillowing her chin on her hands, she watched the water until the boats sailed away, until the sea was empty, and the shadows grew long.

She pushed up, sat back on her heels and lifted her face to the sky. "And that is the first time in too long that I've done nothing at all for an afternoon." She let out a long, contented breath. "It was glorious."

She rose, stretched her arms high, turned. And nearly stumbled over the edge of the cliff.

She would have fallen if he hadn't moved quickly, so quickly she had no sense of him moving at all. But his hands closed firmly over her arms and pulled her to safe ground.

"Steady," he said, and it was more an order than a suggestion.

He might have been the prince of any woman's imaginings. Or the dark angel of her most secret dreams. His hair was black as a moonless night and flew around a face lightly gilded by the sun. A face of strong, sharp bones, of firm, unsmiling mouth, of haunting male beauty.

He was tall. She had only a sense of height as her head reeled. For he had the eyes of the wolf she'd thought she'd seen—tawny and gold, unblinking and intense—under arched brows as black as his hair. They stared directly into hers, making the blood rush hot through her veins. She felt the strength of his hands as he'd yet to release her, thought she saw both impatience and curiosity flicker over that gorgeous face.

But she might have been wrong because he continued to stare, and say nothing.

"I was—you startled me. I didn't hear you. You were just there." She nearly winced as she heard herself babble.

Which was his own fault, he supposed. He could have made her aware of him gradually. But something about the way she'd been lying on the rocks, gazing out at nothing with a half smile on her face had muddled his mind.

"You didn't hear because you were daydreaming." He arched one sweeping black eyebrow. "And talking to yourself."

"Oh. It's a bad habit of mine—talking to myself. Nervous habit."

"Why are you nervous?"

"I'm not—I wasn't." God, she'd tremble in a moment if he didn't let her go. It had been a long, long time since she'd been this close to a man other than Alan. And much too long since she'd felt any kind of response to one. She'd never experienced a reaction this strong, this violent or this disorienting, and put it down to nearly tumbling over a cliff.

"You weren't." He skimmed his hands down to her wrists, felt the jittery bump of her pulse. "Now you are."

"You startled me, as I said." It was an effort, but she glanced over her shoulder and down. "And it's a long drop."

"It is that." He tugged her away another two steps. "Better?"

"Yes, well…I'm Rowan Murray, I'm using Belinda Malone's cabin for a while." She would have offered a hand to shake, but it would have been impossible as he was still cuffing her wrists.

"Donovan. Liam Donovan." He said it quietly, while his thumbs stroked over her pulse beat and somehow steadied it.

"But you're not from around here."

"Aren't I?"

"I mean, your accent. It's beautifully Irish."

When his lips curved and his eyes smiled she very nearly sighed like a teenager faced with a rock star. "I'm from Mayo, but I've had this place as mine for nearly a year now. My cabin's less than a half-mile from Belinda's."

"You know her then?"

"Aye, well enough. We're in the way of being relations, distant ones." His smile was gone now. Her eyes were as blue as the wild bellflowers that grew in sunny patches of the forest in high summer. And in them he found no guile at all. "She didn't tell me to expect a neighbor."

"I suppose she didn't think of it. She didn't tell me to expect one, either." Her hands were free now, though she could still feel the warmth of his fingers, like bracelets around her wrists. "What do you do up here?"

"As I choose. You'll be wanting to do the same. It'll be a good change for you."

"Excuse me?"

"You haven't done what you pleased often enough, have you, Rowan Murray?"

She shivered once and slipped her hands into her pockets. The sun was dipping down toward the horizon and was reason enough for the sudden chill. "I guess I'll have to be careful what I talk to myself about with a quiet-footed neighbor around."

"Nearly a half-mile between us should be enough. I like my solitude." He said it firmly, and though it was ridiculous, it seemed to Rowan he wasn't speaking to her, but to someone, something in the darkening woods beyond. Then his gaze shifted back to her face, held. "I won't infringe on yours."

"I didn't mean to be unfriendly." She tried a smile, wishing she hadn't spoken so abruptly and irritated him. "I've always lived in the city—with so many neighbors I barely notice any of them."

"It doesn't suit you," he said half to himself.

"What?"

"The city. It doesn't suit you or you wouldn't be here, would you?" And what in bloody hell did it matter to him what suited her? he asked himself. She'd be nothing to him unless he decided differently.

"I'm…just taking a little time."

"Aye, well there's plenty of it here. Do you know your way back?"

"Back? Oh, to the cabin? Yes. I take the path to the right then follow the stream."

"Don't linger long." He turned and started down, pausing only briefly to glance up at her. "Night comes quickly here this time of year, and it's easy to be lost in the dark. In the unfamiliar."

"No, I'll start back soon. Mr. Donovan—Liam?"

He stopped again, his gaze clear enough that she caught the quick shadow of impatience in it. "Yes?"

"I was wondering...where's your dog?"

His grin was so fast, so bright and amused that she found herself beaming back at him. "I've no dog."

"But I thought—are there other cabins nearby?"

"Not for three miles and more. We're what's here, Rowan. And what lives in the forest between us." He saw her glance uneasily at the verge of trees and softened. "Nothing that's there will harm you. Enjoy your walk, and your evening. And your time."

Before she could think of another way to stop him, he'd stepped into and been swallowed up by the trees. It was then she noticed just how quickly twilight had fallen, just how chilly the air and how brisk the wind. Abandoning pride, she scrambled down the cliff path and called out to him.

"Liam? Wait a minute, would you? I'll walk back with you for a bit."

But her own voice echoed back to her, turning her throat dry. She moved quickly down the path certain she'd catch a glimpse of him in the trees. There was nothing now but deep shadow.

"Not only quiet," she mumbled, "but fast. Okay, okay." To bolster herself she paused to take three deep breaths. "There's nothing in here that wasn't here when there was more light. Just go back the way you came and stop being an idiot."

But the deeper she went, the thicker the shadows. Like a tide, a thin ground fog slid over the path, white as smoke. She would have sworn she heard music, like bells—or laughter. It harmonized with the sound of the water bubbling over rocks, whispered in counterpoint to the *whoosh* and sigh of the wind in the trees.

A radio, she thought. Or a television. Sounds carried oddly in some places. Liam had turned on music, and for some reason she could hear it playing. It only seemed as if it was just ahead of her, in the direction of her own cabin. The wind played tricks.

The sigh of relief as she came to the last bend of the stream froze in her throat as she saw the glint of gold eyes peering out of the shadows. Then with a rustle of leaves, they were gone.

Rowan increased her pace to a jog and didn't break stride until she'd reached the door. She didn't start breathing again until she was inside and the door was securely locked behind her.

She moved quickly, switching on lights until the first floor of the cabin blazed with them. Then she poured herself a glass from one of the bottles of wine she'd brought along, lifted it in a toast and swallowed deep.

"To strange beginnings, mysterious neighbors and invisible dogs."

To make herself feel more at home, she heated a can of soup and ate it standing up, dreaming, looking out the kitchen window, as she often did in her apartment in the city.

But the dreams were softer here, and yet more clear. Towering trees and bubbling water, thrashing waves and the last light of the day.

A handsome man with tawny eyes who stood on a windswept cliff and smiled at her.

She sighed, wishing she'd been clever and polished, had known a way to flirt lightly, speak casually so that he might have looked at her with interest rather than annoyance and amusement.

Which was ridiculous, she reminded herself, as Liam Donovan wasn't wasting his time thinking of her at all. So it was pointless to think of him.

Following habit, she tidied up, switching off lights as she moved upstairs. There she indulged herself by filling the wonderfully deep claw-foot tub with hot water and fragrant bubbles, settling into it with a sigh, a book and a second glass of wine.

She immediately decided this was a luxury she hadn't allowed herself nearly often enough.

"That's going to change." She slid back, moaning with pleasure. "So many things are going to change. I just have to think of them all."

When the water turned tepid, she climbed out to change into the cozy flannel pajamas she'd bought. Another indulgence was to light the bedroom fire, then crawl under the cloud-light duvet beneath the canopy and snuggle into her book.

Within ten minutes, she was asleep, with her reading glasses sliding down her nose, the lights on and the last of her wine going warm in her glass.

She dreamed of a sleek black wolf who padded silently into her room, watching her out of curious gold eyes as she slept. It seemed he spoke to her—his mind to her mind.

I wasn't looking for you. I wasn't waiting for you. I don't want what you're bringing me. Go back to your safe world, Rowan Murray. Mine isn't for you.

She couldn't answer but to think *I only want time. I'm only looking for time.*

He came close to the bed, so that her hand nearly brushed his head. *If you take it here, it may trap us both. Is that a risk you're willing to take?*

Oh, she wanted to touch, to feel, and with a sigh slid her hand over the warm fur, let her fingers dive into it. *It's time I took one.*

Under her hand wolf became man. His breath fluttered over her face as he leaned close, so close. "If I kissed you now, Rowan, what might happen?"

Her body seemed to shimmer with that sudden raw need. She moaned with it, arched, reached out.

Liam only laid a finger on her lips. "Sleep," he told her and slipped the glasses off, laid them on the table beside her. He switched off the light, closed his hand into a fist as the urge to touch her, to really touch her, lanced through him.

"Damn it. I don't want this. I don't want her."

He flung up his hand and vanished.

Later, much later, she dreamed of a wolf, black as midnight on the cliffs over the sea. With his head thrown back he called to the swimming moon.

Chapter 2

It became a habit over the next few days for Rowan to look for the wolf. She would see him, most often early in the morning or just before twilight, standing at the edge of the trees.

Watching the house, she thought. Watching her.

She realized, on those mornings when she didn't see him, that she was disappointed. So much so that she began leaving food out in hopes to lure him closer, to keep him a regular visitor in what she was starting to consider her little world.

He was on her mind quite a bit. Nearly every morning she woke with fading snippets of dreams just at the edge of her mind. Dreams where he sat by her bed while she slept, where she sometimes roused just enough to reach out and stroke that soft silky fur or feel the strong ridge of muscle along his back.

Now and then, the wolf became mixed in her

dreams with her neighbor. On those mornings, she climbed out of sleep with her system still quivering from an aching sexual frustration that baffled and embarrassed her.

When she was logical, she could remind herself that Liam Donovan was the only human being she'd seen in the best part of a week. As a sample of the species, he was spectacular and the perfect fodder for erotic dreams.

But all in all she preferred thinking of the wolf, weaving a story about him. She liked pretending he was her guardian, protecting her from any evil spirits that lived in the forest.

She spent most of her time reading or sketching, or taking long walks. And trying not to think that it was nearly time to make her promised weekly call home to her parents.

She often heard music, drifting through the woods or in through her windows. Pipes and flutes, bells and strings. Once there was harpsong so sweet and so pure that it made her throat ache with tears.

While she wallowed in the peace, the solitude, the lack of demand on her time and attention, there were also moments of loneliness so acute it hurt the heart. Even when the need for another voice, for human contact pulled at her, she couldn't quite gather the courage, or find a reasonable excuse, to seek out Liam.

To offer him a cup of coffee, she thought as twilight slipped through the trees and there was no sign of her wolf. Or maybe a hot meal. A little conversation, she mused, absently twisting the tip of her braid around her finger.

"Doesn't he ever get lonely?" she wondered. "What does he do all day, all night?"

The wind rose, and in the distance thunder mumbled. A storm brewing, she thought, moving to the door to fling it open to the fast, cool air. Looking up, she watched dark clouds roll and bump, caught the faint blink of far-off lightning.

She thought it would be lovely to sleep with the sound of rain falling on the roof. Better, to curl up in bed with a book and read half the night while the wind howled and the rain lashed.

Smiling at the idea, she shifted her gaze. And looked directly into the glinting eyes of the wolf.

She stumbled back a step, pressing a hand to her throat where her heart had leaped. He was halfway across the clearing, closer than he'd ever come. Wiping her nervous hands on her jeans, she cautiously stepped out on the porch.

"Hello." She laughed a little, but kept one hand firmly on the doorknob. Just in case. "You're so beautiful," she murmured while he stood, still as a stone carving. "I look for you every day. You never eat the food I leave out. Nothing else does, either. I'm not a very good cook. I keep wishing you'd come closer."

As her pulse began to level, she lowered slowly into a crouch. "I won't hurt you," she murmured. "I've been reading about wolves. Isn't it odd that I brought a book about you with me? I don't even remember packing it, but I brought so many books. You shouldn't be interested in me," she said with a sigh. "You should be running with a pack, with your mate."

The sadness hit so quickly, so sharply, that she closed her eyes against it. "Wolves mate for life," she said quietly, then jolted when lightning slashed and the bellow of thunder answered by shaking the sky.

The clearing was empty. The black wolf was gone. Rowan walked to the porch rocker, sat and curled up her legs to watch the rain sweep in.

He was thinking about her far too much and far too often. It infuriated him. Liam was a man who prided himself on self-control. When one possessed power, control must walk with it. Power untempered could corrupt. It could destroy.

He'd been taught from birth his responsibilities as well as his advantages. His gifts as well as his curses. Solitude was his way of escaping all of it, at least for short spans of time.

He knew, too well, no one escaped destiny.

The son of princes was expected to accept destiny.

Alone in his cabin, he thought of her. The way she'd looked when he'd come into the clearing. The way fear had danced around her even as she'd stepped outside.

There was such sweetness in her, it pulled at him, even as he struggled to stay away. She thought she was putting him at ease, letting him grow accustomed to her by leaving him food. Speaking to him in that quiet voice that trembled with nerves.

He wondered how many other women, alone in what was essentially wilderness, would have the courage or the desire to talk to a wolf, much less reassure him.

She thought she was a coward—he'd touched her mind gently, but enough to scan her thoughts. She didn't have any concept of what she had inside her, hadn't explored it, or been allowed to.

Strong sense of family, great loyalty and pitifully low self-esteem.

He shook his head as he sipped coffee and watched the storm build. What in Finn's name was he supposed to do about her?

If it had just been a matter of giving her subtle little pushes to discover herself and her own powers, that would have been…interesting, he supposed. He might have enjoyed the task. But he knew it was a great deal more.

He'd been shown just enough to worry him.

If she'd been sent to him and he accepted her, took her, the decision he'd left home and family to make would be made for him.

She was not one of his kind.

Yet already there were needs stirring. She was a lovely woman after all, vulnerable, a little lost. Those needs would have been natural enough, particularly after his long, self-imposed solitude.

Male required female.

But the needs were deeper, stronger and more demanding than he'd experienced before, and that he cared to experience. When you felt too much, control slipped. Without control, there was no choice. He'd taken this year to himself to make choices.

Yet he couldn't stay away from her. He'd been wise enough, he considered, to keep his distance in this form—at least when she was awake and aware. Still he was drawn through the forest to watch her, to listen to her mind. Or to sit alone here in this room, cast the fire and study her in the flames.

Love waits.

He set his teeth, set his cup down with a snap of china on wood as the whisper floated over him. "Damn it, I'll deal with it, with her. In my own time. In my own way. Leave me be."

In the dark window glass his own reflection faded, replaced by a woman with tumbling gold hair and eyes of the same rich color, who smiled softly. "Liam," she said. "Stubborn you are, and always were."

He cocked a brow. "Mother, 'tis easy when you learn from the best."

She laughed, eyes sparkling against the night. "That's true enough—if you're speaking of your Da. The storm breaks, and she's alone. Will you leave her that way?"

"It's best for both of us if I do just that. She's not one of us."

"Liam, when you're ready, you'll look into her heart, and into your own. Trust what you find." Then she sighed, knowing her son would follow his own path as always. "I'll give your father your best."

"Do. I love you."

"I know it. Come home soon, Liam of Donovan. We're missing you."

As her image faded, lightning slashed out of the sky, driving down like a lance to stab the ground. It left no mark, no burn, even as thunder roared behind it; Liam understood it was his father's way of echoing his wife's words.

"All right then. Bloody hell. I'll have a look and see how well she's riding out the storm."

He turned, focused, then flicked a wrist, jabbing a finger at the cold hearth. The fire leaped, though there was no log, no kindling to burn.

"Lightning flares and thunder moans. How does the woman fare alone? Chill the fire to let me see. As I will, so mote it be."

He dipped his hands into his pockets as the flames settled, steadied. In the cool gold light, shadows shifted, parted, then opened to him.

He saw her carrying a candle through the dark, her face pale in its flickering light, her eyes wide. She fumbled through drawers in her kitchen, talking to herself, as she was prone to. And jolted like a frightened deer when the next flash of lightning broke the night.

Well, he hadn't thought of that, Liam admitted, and in a rare show of frustration, dragged a hand through his hair. Her power was out, and she was alone in the dark, and scared half to death. Hadn't Belinda told her how to work the little generator, or where the flashlight was? The emergency lanterns?

Apparently not.

He could hardly leave her there, could he? Shivering and stumbling around. Which, he supposed with a sour smile, was exactly what his clever, meddling cousin had known.

He'd make sure she had light, and heat, but that would be the end of it. He wouldn't linger.

While he was a witch, he was also a man. And both parts of him wanted her entirely too much for comfort.

"Just a storm, it's just a storm. No big deal." Rowan all but chanted the words as she lighted more candles.

She wasn't afraid of the dark, not really. But it was so *damn* dark, and the lightning had struck so close to the cabin. The thunder rattled the windows until she was certain they would just explode.

And if she hadn't been sitting outside, daydreaming while the storm blew in, she'd have had a fire built. She'd have the warmth and light from that *and* the candlelight, and it would be sort of…cozy. If she really worked on believing it.

And now the power was out, the phones were out and the storm appeared to be at its peak directly over her pretty little cabin.

There were candles, she reminded herself. Dozens and dozens of candles. White ones, blue ones, red ones, green ones. She could only think that Belinda had bought out some candle store. Some were so lovely, with odd and beautiful symbols carved into them, that she held back from lighting them. And after all, she must have fifty flaring away by now, giv-

ing adequate light and offering marvelous scents to
settle the nerves.

"Okay. All right." She set yet one more candle on
the table in front of the sofa and rubbed her chilled
hands. "I ought to be able to see enough to get a fire
going. Then I'll just curl up right here on the couch
and wait it out. It'll be fine."

But even as she crouched in front of the hearth and
began to arrange the kindling, the wind howled. Her
door banged open like a bullet out of a gun and half
the cheery candles behind her blew out.

She leaped up, whirled around. And screamed.

Liam stood a few paces away, the wind swirling
through his hair, the candlelight gleaming in his eyes.
She dropped kindling on her stockinged feet, yelped
and fell backward into a chair.

"I seem to have startled you again," he said in that
mild and beautiful voice. "Sorry."

"I—you. God! The door…"

"It's open." He turned, crossed to it and closed
out the wind and rain.

She'd been certain she'd locked it when she'd
rushed in out of the storm. Obviously not, she thought
now and did her best to swallow her heart and get it
back in its proper place.

"I thought you might have been having some trouble with the storm." He stepped toward her, each
movement graceful as a dancer's. Or a stalking wolf.
"It seems I was right."

"Power's out," she managed.

"So I see. You're cold." He picked up the scattered kindling and crouched to build a fire with wood

and match. He thought she'd had enough surprises for one night, even if it did take quite a bit longer that way.

"I wanted to get some light before I built a fire. Belinda has a lot of candles."

"Naturally." The kindling caught with a quick crackle, and flames licked obligingly at the logs he arranged. "This'll warm the room soon. There's a small generator out back. I can start it for you if you like, but this will pass before long."

He stayed where he was, with the firelight dancing over his face. And looking at him, she forgot about the storm and fears of the dark. She wondered if all that gorgeous hair that fell nearly to his shoulders was as soft as it looked, wondered why it seemed she knew exactly how it would feel under her fingers.

Why she had an image of him leaning over her, leaning close, with his mouth a breath away from hers. Only a breath away.

"You're daydreaming again, Rowan."

"Oh." She blinked, flushed, shook herself clear. "Sorry. The storm's made me jumpy. Would you like some wine?" She pushed herself up, began backing quickly toward the kitchen. "I have a very nice Italian white I tried last night. I'll just...pour some. Won't be a minute."

For Lord's sake, for Lord's sake, she berated herself as she dashed into the kitchen where a half-dozen candles glowed on the counter. Why did being around him make her so skittish and stupid! She'd been alone with attractive men before. She was a grown woman, wasn't she?

She got the bottle out of the refrigerator by the light of the candles, found glasses and filled them. When she turned, a glass in each hand, he was there just there behind her, and she jolted.

Wine sloshed over the rim and onto the back of her hand.

"*Must* you do that!" She snapped it out before she could stop herself, then watched that fast, fabulous grin flash over his face, bright and blinding as the lightning in the storm.

"I suppose not." Ah, the hell with it, he decided. He was entitled to some small pleasures. With his eyes on hers, he lifted her damp hand, bent his head and slowly licked.

The best she could manage was a small, quiet moan.

"You're right. It's very nice wine." He took the glass and when her freed hand fell limply to her side, smiled. Sipped. "You've a lovely face, Rowan Murray. I've thought of it since last I saw you."

"You have?"

"Did you think I wouldn't?"

She was so obviously befuddled it was tempting to press his advantage, to go with the urge grinding in him to take before she knew all he wanted, and what he refused to want. One step closer, he mused, the slow slide of his fingers around the base of her neck where the flesh was warm and smooth. Fragile. His mouth to hers while the taste of her was still mixed with the wine on his tongue.

And he wouldn't be in the mood to leave it at something quite so simple, or quite so innocent.

"Come in by the fire." He stepped back to give her room to pass. "Where it's warmer."

She recognized the ache spreading inside her. The same ache, she thought, as she woke with whenever she dreamed of him. She moved past him, into the living room, praying she could think of something to say that wouldn't sound idiotic.

"If you came here to relax," he began with just a hint of impatience in his voice, "you're doing a preciously poor job of it. Sit down and stop fretting. The storm won't stay long, and neither will I."

"I like the company. I'm not used to being alone for such long stretches of time."

She sat, managing a smile. But he stood by the fire, leaned against the mantel. He watched her. Watched her in a way that reminded her of—

"Isn't that why you came here?" He said it to interrupt her thoughts before they inched too close to what she wasn't prepared to know. "To have time alone?"

"Yes. And I like it. But it's odd just the same. I was a teacher for a long time. I'm used to having a lot of people around."

"Do you like them?"

"Them? Students?"

"No, people." He made a vague and oddly dismissive gesture with one elegant hand. "In general."

"Why…yes." She laughed a little, leaning back in her chair without being aware her shoulders had lost their knots of tension. "Don't you?"

"Not particularly—as a rule." He took a sip of wine, reflecting. "So many of them are demanding, selfish, self-absorbed. And while that's not so much of a problem, they often hurt each other quite consciously, quite carelessly. There's no point, and there should be no pride in causing harm.''

''Most people don't mean to.'' She saw the light in his eye and shook her head. ''Oh, you're cynical. I can't understand cynics.''

''That's because you're a romantic, and a naive one at that. But it's charming on you.''

''Now, should I be flattered or insulted?'' she wondered aloud, smiling with more ease than she'd ever felt with him, even when he moved to sit at the ottoman in front of her chair.

''Truth can be accepted without either. What do you teach?''

''Literature—or I used to.''

''That would explain the books.'' They were stacked on the coffee table and in a box beside the couch. He'd seen others piled on the kitchen table and knew there were still more in her bedroom upstairs.

''Reading's one of my greatest pleasures. I love sliding into a story.''

''But this...'' He leaned back, reached over and plucked up the top book on the table. ''*The Study of Wolves, Their History and Habits.* That wouldn't be a story, would it?''

''No. I bought that on impulse one day, and didn't even realize I'd packed it. But I'm glad I did.'' In a habitual gesture she brushed at the hair that had come loose from her braid. ''You must have seen him.'' She eased forward, the delight in her large, dark eyes nearly irresistible. "The black wolf that comes around."

He continued to look into her eyes, straight in as he enjoyed his wine. "I can't say I have."

"Oh, but I've seen him nearly every day since I came. He's gorgeous, and doesn't seem as wary of people as you'd expect. He came into the clearing right before the storm tonight. And sometimes I hear him calling, or it seems I do. Haven't you?"

"I'm closer to the sea," he told her. "That's what I listen to. A wolf is a wild thing, Rowan, as I'm sure your book has told you. And a rogue, one who runs alone, the wildest of all."

"I wouldn't want to tame him. I'd say we're just curious about each other at this point." She glanced toward the window, wondered if the wolf had found a warm dry place for the night. "They don't hunt for sport," she added, absently tossing her braid behind her back. "Or out of viciousness. They hunt to feed. Most often they live in packs, families. Protect their young, and—" She broke off, jumping a little when lightning flashed bright and close.

"Nature's a violent thing. It only tolerates the rest of us. Nature can be generous or ruthless." He put the book aside. "You have to have a care how you deal with it, and you'll never understand it."

Their knees were brushing, their bodies close. She caught the scent of him, sharply male, almost animal, and absolutely dangerous. His lips curved in a smile as he nodded. "Exactly so," he murmured, then set his glass aside and rose. "I'll start the generator for you. You'll be happier with some electricity."

"Yes, I suppose you're right." She got to her feet, wondering why her heart was pounding. It had nothing to do with the storm raging outside now, and everything to do with the one so suddenly brewing inside her. "Thank you for helping."

"It's not a problem." He wasn't going to let it be a problem. "It'll only be a moment." Briefly, lightly, his fingers danced over the back of her hand. "It was good wine," he murmured, and walked out to the kitchen.

It took her ten long seconds to get her breath back, to lower the hand she'd pressed to her cheek and follow him. Just as she stepped into the kitchen, the lights flashed on, making her yelp. Even as she laughed at herself, she wondered how the man moved so fast. The kitchen was empty, her lights were on, and it was as if he'd never been there.

She pulled open the back door and winced when the wind and rain lashed at her. Shivering a little, she leaned out. "Liam?" But there was nothing but the rain and the dark. "Don't go," she murmured, leaning on the doorjamb as the rain soaked her shirt. "Please don't leave me alone."

The next burst of lightning shot the forest into bright relief. And gleamed off the coat of the wolf that stood in the driving rain at the foot of the steps.

"God." She fumbled on the wall for the light switch, flicked it and had the floodlights pouring on. He was still there, his coat gleaming with wet, his eyes patiently watching. She moistened her lips, took a slow step back. "You should come in out of the rain."

A thrill sprinted up her spine as he leaped gracefully onto the porch. She didn't realize she was holding her breath until his damp fur brushed her leg as he walked inside, and she released it with a shiver.

"Well." Trembling a little, she turned so they watched each other. "There's a wolf in the house. An incredibly handsome wolf," she murmured and found herself not thinking twice about shutting the door and closing them inside together. "Um, I'm going to go in..." She gestured vaguely. "There. It's warm. You can—"

She broke off, charmed and baffled when he simply swung around and stalked through the doorway. She followed to see him walk to the fire, settle himself then look back at her as if waiting.

"Smart, aren't you?" she murmured. "Very smart." As she approached cautiously, his gaze never left her face. She lowered herself to the ottoman. "Do you belong to anyone?" She lifted her hand, her fingers itching to touch. She waited for a growl, a snarl, a warning, and when none came she lightly laid her hand on his head. "No, you wouldn't belong to anyone but yourself. That's how it is for the brave and the beautiful."

When her fingers stroked down to his neck, rubbing gently, his eyes narrowed. She thought she recognized pleasure in them and smiled a little. "You like that? Me, too. Touching's as good as being touched, and no one's really touched me for so long. But you don't want to hear the story of my life. It's not very interesting. Yours would be," she mused. "I bet you'd have fascinating tales to tell."

He smelled of the forest, of the rain. Of animal. And oddly, of something...familiar. She grew bolder, running her hands down his back, over his flanks, back to his head. "You'll dry here by the fire," she began, then her hand paused in midstroke, her brows drew together.

"He wasn't wet," she said quietly. "He came through the rain, but he wasn't wet. Was he?" Puzzled, she stared out the dark window. Liam's hair was as black as the wolf's fur, but it hadn't gleamed with rain or damp. Had it?

"How could that be? Even if he'd driven over he had to get from a car to the door, and..."

She trailed off when the wolf moved closer, when his handsome head nuzzled her thigh. With a murmur of pleasure, she began to stroke him again, grinning when the rumble in his throat reminded her of a very human, very male sound of approval.

"Maybe you're lonely, too."

And she sat with him while the storm shifted out to sea, the thunder quieted, and the whips of rain and wind turned to soft patters.

It didn't surprise her that he walked through the house with her. Somehow it seemed perfectly natural that he would accompany her as she blew out candles, switched off lights. He climbed the stairs with her and sat by her side as she lighted the bedroom fire.

"I love it here," she murmured, sitting back on her heels to watch the flames catch. "Even when I'm lonely, like I was tonight, it feels right being here. As if I've always needed to come to this place."

She turned her head, smiled a little. They were eye

to eye now, deep blue to dark gold. Reaching out she skimmed her hand under his powerful jaw, rubbing the silky line of his throat. "No one would believe me. No one I know would believe me if I told them I was in a cabin in Oregon talking to a big, black, gorgeous wolf. And maybe I'm just dreaming. I do a lot of that," she added as she rose. "Maybe everyone's right and I do too much dreaming."

She crossed to the dresser and took a pair of pajamas from the drawer. "I guess it's pretty pitiful when your dreams are the most interesting part of your life. I really want to change that. I don't mean I have to climb mountains or jump out of planes..."

He stopped listening—and he had listened all along. But now, as she spoke, she tugged the navy sweatshirt she wore over her head and began to unbutton the simple plaid shirt beneath.

He stopped hearing the words as she slipped the shirt off, stood folding the sweatshirt wearing only a lacy white bra and jeans.

She was small and slender, her skin milk pale. Her jeans bagged a bit at the waist, making the man inside the wolf nearly groan as her fingers reached for the button. His blood warmed, his pulse quickened as she let the denim slide carelessly down her legs.

The swatch of white rode low on her hips. He wanted his mouth there, just there along that lovely curve. To taste the flesh, to feel the shape of bone. And to slide his tongue under the white until she quivered.

She sat, tugging off her socks, shaking her feet free

of the jeans. And nearly drove him mad as she stood
to lay them aside.

The low growl in his throat went unnoticed by both
of them as she unhooked her bra in an innocent strip-
tease. He felt his control slipping as he imagined cup-
ping his hands there, over small white breasts, skimming his thumbs over pale pink nipples.

Lowering his head until his mouth was—

The sudden violent slash of lightning had her jumping, muffling a scream. "God! The storm must be
coming back. I thought…" She stopped in midsent-
ence as she glanced over, saw those gold eyes glinting. In an instinctive gesture, she crossed her arms
over her naked breasts. Beneath them her heart
bounced like a rabbit.

His eyes looked so…human, she thought with a
quick panic. The expression in them hungry. "Why
do I suddenly feel like Little Red Riding Hood?" She
eased out a breath, drew in another. "That's just foolish." But her voice wasn't quite steady as she made
the grab for her pajama top. She made a little squeak
of surprise when he caught the dangling sleeve in his
teeth and dragged it away.

A laugh bubbled up and out. She grabbed the collar
of the flannel, pulled. The quick, unexpected tug-of-
war made her laugh again. "You think it's funny?"
she demanded. Damn if she didn't see amusement in
those fascinating eyes. "I just bought these. They
may not be pretty, but they're warm—and it's cold in
here. Now, let go!"

When he did, abruptly, she stumbled back two
paces before she caught her balance. Wonderfully na-

ked but for that triangle at her hips, she narrowed her eyes at him. "A real joker, aren't you?" She held the top up, searching for tears or teeth marks, and found none. "Well, at least you didn't eat it."

He watched her slip it on, button it. There was something erotic even in that, in the way the brightly patterned flannel skimmed her thighs. But before she could pull on the bottoms he pleased himself by shifting his head, running his tongue from her ankle to the back of her knee.

She chuckled, bent down to scratch his ears as though he were the family dog. "I like you, too." After pulling the bottoms on, she reached up to loosen what was left of her braid. As she reached for her brush, the wolf padded over to the bed, leaped up and stretched out at the foot.

"Oh, I don't think so." Amused, she turned, running the brush through her hair. "I really don't. You'll have to get down from there."

He watched her unblinkingly. She would have sworn he smiled. Huffing out a breath, she shook her hair back, set the brush aside, then walked to the side of the bed. In her best teacher's voice she ordered him down and pointed meaningfully at the floor.

This time she *knew* he smiled.

"You're not sleeping in the bed." She reached out, intended to pull him off. But when he bared his teeth, she cleared her throat. "Well, one night. What could it hurt?"

Watching him cautiously, she climbed up, sliding under the duvet. He simply lay, his head snugged between his front paws. She picked up her glasses, her book, shrugging when the wolf lay still. Satisfied, she piled the pillows behind her and settled in to read.

Only moments later, the mattress shifted, and the wolf moved over to lie at her side, laying his head in her lap. Without a thought, Rowan stroked him and began to read aloud.

She read until her eyes grew heavy, her voice thick, and once more slipped into sleep with a book in her hand.

The air quivered as wolf became man. Liam touched a finger to her forehead. "Dream, Rowan," he murmured, pausing as he felt her slide deeper. He took her book, her glasses and set them neatly on the bedside table. Then he eased her down, lifting her head so he could spread out the pillows.

"You must be waking every morning stiff as a board," he murmured. "Forever falling asleep sitting up." He skimmed the back of his hand over her cheek, then sighed.

The scent of her, silky and female and subtle was enough to drive him mad. Each quiet breath through those full and parted lips was a kind of invitation.

"Damn it, Rowan, you lie in bed with me with the rain on the roof and read Yeats aloud in that soft, almost prim voice of yours. How should I resist that? I'll have to have you sooner or later. Later's the better for both of us. But I need something tonight."

He took her hand, pressed palm to palm, linked fingers. And shut his eyes. "Come with me, two minds, one dream. Sleep is not now what it seems. Give what I need, and take what you'll have from me. As I will, so mote it be."

She moaned. And moved. Her free arm flung up over her head, her lips parting on a shuddering breath that seemed to whisper in his blood. His own pulse thickened as he made love to her with his mind. Tasted her, touched her with his thoughts. Gave himself to hers.

Lost in dreams, she arched up, her body shuddering under phantom hands.

She smelled him, that musky, half-animal scent that had already stirred her more than once in dreams. Images, sensations, desires, confused and tangled and arousing beyond belief swarmed through her. Embracing them, she murmured his name and opened to him, body and mind.

The hot wave of his thoughts lifted her up, held her trembling, aching, quivering, then stabbed her with unspeakable pleasure. She heard her name, said quietly, almost desperately. Repeated. Desire drugged the mind, swirled through it, then slid silently away into fulfillment.

He sat, his eyes still closed, his hand still joined with hers. Listened to the rain, her soft and steady breathing. Resisting the urge to lie with her, to touch her now with more than his mind, he threw his head back. And vanished.

Chapter 3

She woke early, blissfully relaxed. Her body seemed to glow. Her mind was calm, clear and content. Rowan was out of bed and in the shower before she remembered anything. Then with a muttered curse, she jumped out, dripping, grabbed a towel and dashed back into the bedroom.

The bed was empty. There was no beautiful wolf curled in front of the cold fire. Ignoring the water sliding down her legs she dashed downstairs, searching the house and leaving a trail of damp behind her.

The kitchen door hung open, letting in the chill of the morning. Still she stepped out, her cold toes curling up in protest as she scanned the line of trees.

How did he get out—and where did he go? she wondered. Since when do wolves open doors?

She hadn't imagined it. No, she refused to believe that her imagination could create such clear images, such textures, such events. That would make her crazy, wouldn't it? she thought with a half laugh as she backed inside again and closed the door.

The wolf had been in the house. He'd sat with her, stayed with her. Even slept on the bed. She could remember exactly the feel of his fur, the scent of rain and wild on it, the expressions in his eyes, and the warmth, the simple comfort, when he'd laid his head on her lap.

However…unusual the evening, it had happened. However odd her own actions, letting him in, petting him, she had done so.

And if she'd had a brain cell in her head, she'd have thought to grab her camera and take a few pictures of him.

To prove what? To show to whom? The wolf, she realized, was her personal and private joy. She didn't want to share him.

She went back upstairs, back to the shower, wondering how long it would be before he came back.

She caught herself singing and grinned. She couldn't remember ever waking up happier or with more energy. And wasn't that part of the plan? she thought as she lifted her face to the spray and let the hot water stream. To find out just what made her happy. If it happened to be spending a stormy night with a wolf, so what?

"Try to explain that one, Rowan." Laughing at herself, she toweled off. Humming, she started to wipe the steam from the bathroom mirror, then paused, staring at her own misty reflection.

Did she look different? she wondered, leaning

closer to study her face, the glow of her skin, the sleek sheen of wet hair, and most of all the light in her eyes.

What had put that there? She lifted her hand, running her fingers curiously along the ridge of her cheekbones just under her eyes.

Dreams. And her fingers trembled lightly as she dropped them. Hot and shivering dreams. Colors and shapes pulsing through her mind, through her body. So stunning, so...erotic. Hands on her breasts, but not. A mouth crushing down on hers but never really touching.

Closing her eyes, she let the towel fall, skimmed her hands over her breasts, down, up again, trying to focus on where she had journeyed in sleep.

The taste of male skin, the hot slide of it over her own. Needs rocketing through the mind to be met and met again until the beauty of it brought tears.

She'd never experienced anything like that, not even in life. How could she find it in dreams?

And why should she go to sleep with a wolf and dream of a man.

Of Liam.

She knew it had been Liam. She could all but feel the shape of his mouth on hers. But how could that be? she wondered, tracing a fingertip over her lips. How could she be so sure she knew just what it would be like to meet his mouth with hers.

"Because you want to," she murmured, opening her eyes to meet those in the mirror again. "Because you want him and you've never wanted anyone else like this. And, Rowan, you moron, you don't have the slightest idea how to make it happen, except in dreams. So that's where it happens for you. Psychology 101—real basic stuff.''

Not certain if she should be amused or appalled at herself, she dressed, went down to brew her morning coffee. Snug in her sweater, she flung open the windows to the cool, fresh air left behind by the rain.

She thought, without enthusiasm, about cereal or toast or yogurt. She had a yen for chocolate chip cookies, which was absurd at barely eight in the morning, so she told herself. Dutifully she opened the cupboard for cereal, then slammed it shut.

If she wanted cookies, she was having them. And with a grin on her face and a gleam in her eye, began to drag out ingredients. She slopped flour, scattered sugar on the counter. And mixed with abandon. There was no one to see her lick dough from her fingers. No one to gently remind her that she should tidy up between each step of the process.

She made an unholy mess.

Dancing with impatience, she waited for the first batch to bake. "Come on, come on. I've got to have one." The minute the buzzer went off, she grabbed the cookie sheet out, dropped it on the top of the stove, then scooped up the first cookie with a spatula. She blew on it, slipped it off and tossed it from hand to hand. Still she burned her tongue on hot, gleaming chocolate as she bit in. And rolling her eyes dramatically, she swallowed with a hedonistic groan.

"Good job. Really good job. More."

She ate a dozen before the second batch was baked.

It felt decadent, childish. And wonderful.

When the phone rang, she popped the next batch in, and lifted the receiver with doughy fingers. "Hello?"

"Rowan. Good morning."

For a moment the voice meant nothing to her, then with a guilty start she realized it was Alan. "Good morning."

"I hope I didn't wake you?"

"No, no. I've been up quite a while. I'm..." She grinned and chose another cookie. "Just having breakfast."

"Glad to hear it. You tend to skip too many meals."

She put the whole cookie into her mouth and talked around it. "Not this time. Maybe the mountain air..." She managed to swallow. "Stimulates my appetite."

"You don't sound like yourself."

"Really?" I'm not myself, she wanted to say. I'm better. And I'm not nearly finished yet.

"You sound a little giddy. Are you all right?"

"I'm fine. I'm wonderful." How could she explain to this solid and serious man with his solid and serious voice that she'd been dancing in the kitchen eating cookies, that she'd spent the evening with a wolf, that she'd had erotic dreams about a man she barely knew?

And that she wouldn't change a moment of any of those experiences.

"I'm getting lots of reading done," she said instead. "Taking long walks. I've been doing some sketching, too. I'd forgotten how much I enjoy it. It's a gorgeous morning. The sky's unbelievably blue."

"I checked the weather for your area last night. There were reports of a severe thunderstorm. I tried to call, but your lines were out."

"Yes, we had a storm. That's probably why it's so spectacular this morning."

"I was worried, Rowan. If I hadn't been able to reach you this morning, I was going to fly to Portland and rent a car."

The thought of it, just the thought of him invading her magical little world filled her with panic. She had to fight to keep it out of her voice. "Oh, Alan, there's absolutely no need to worry. I'm fine. The storm was exciting, actually. And I have a generator, emergency lights."

"I don't like thinking of you up there alone, in some rustic little hut in the middle of nowhere. What if you hurt yourself, or fell ill, got a flat tire?"

Her mood began to deflate, degree by degree. She could actually feel the drop. He'd said the same words to her before, and so had her parents, with the exact same tone of bafflement mixed with concern.

"Alan, it's a lovely, sturdy and very spacious cabin, not a hut. I'm only about five miles outside of a very nice little town, which makes this far from the middle of nowhere. If I hurt myself or get sick, I'll go to a doctor. If I get a flat tire, I suppose I'll figure out how to change it."

"You're still alone, Rowan, and as last night proved, easily cut off."

"The phone's working just fine now," she said between clenched teeth. "And I have a cell phone in the Rover. Added to that, I believe I have a moderately intelligent mind, I'm in perfect health, I'm twenty-seven years old and the entire purpose of my coming here was to be alone.''

There was a moment's silence, a moment just long enough to let her know she'd hurt his feelings. And more than long enough to bring her a swift wash of guilt. ''Alan—''

''I'd hoped you'd be ready to come home, but that apparently isn't the case. I miss you, Rowan. Your family misses you. I only wanted to let you know.''

''I'm sorry.'' How many times in her life had she said those words? she wondered as she pressed her fingers to the dull ache forming in her temple. ''I didn't mean to snap at you, Alan. I suppose I feel a little defensive. No, I'm not ready to come back. If you speak to my parents, tell them I'll call them later this evening, and that I'm fine.''

''I'll be seeing your father later today.'' His voice was stiff now, his way—she knew—of letting her know he was hurt. ''I'll tell him. Please keep in touch.''

''I will. Of course, I will. It was nice of you to call. I'll, ah, write you a long letter later this week.''

''I'd enjoy that. Goodbye, Rowan.''

Her cheerful mood totally evaporated, she hung up, turned and looked at the chaos of the kitchen. As penance, she cleaned every inch of it, then put the cookies in a plastic container, sealing them away.

''No, I am not going to brood. Absolutely not.'' She banged open a cupboard door, took out a smaller container and transferred half the cookies into it.

Before she could talk herself out of it, she grabbed

a light jacket from the hook by the door, and tucking the container under her arm, stepped outside.

She didn't have a clue where Liam's cabin was, but he'd said he was closer to the sea. It only made sense to hunt it out, she decided. In case of…an emergency. She'd take a walk, and if she didn't find it… Well, she thought shaking the cookies, she wouldn't starve while she was looking.

She walked into the trees, struck again at how much cooler, how much greener it was inside them. There was birdsong, the whisper of the trees and the sweet smell of pine. Where sunlight could dapple through, it danced on the forest floor, sparkled on the water of the stream.

The deeper she walked, the higher her mood rose again. She paused briefly, just to close her eyes, to let the wind ruffle her hair, play against her cheeks. How could she explain this, just this, to a man like Alan? she wondered. Alan whose every want was logical, whose every step was reasonable and solid.

How could she make him, or anyone else from the world she'd run from, understand what it was like to crave something as intangible as the sound of trees singing, the sharp taste the sea added to the air, the simple peace of standing alone in something so vast and so alive?

"I'm not going back there." The words, more than the sound of her own voice, had her eyes snapping open in surprise. She hadn't realized she'd decided anything, much less something that momentous. The half laugh that escaped was tinged with triumph. "I'm not going back," she repeated. "I don't know where I'm going, but it won't be back."

She laughed again, longer, fuller as she turned a dizzy circle. With a spring to her step, she started to take the curve of the path to the right. Out of the corner of her eye, she saw a flash of white. Turning, she stared with openmouthed wonder at the white doe.

They watched each other with the tumbling stream between them, the doe with serene gold eyes and a hide as white as clouds, and the woman with both shock and awe glowing in her face.

Captivated, Rowan stepped forward. The deer stood, elegant as a sculpture of ice. Then with a lift of her head, she turned fluidly and leaped into the trees. Without a moment's hesitation, Rowan scrambled across the stream, using polished rocks as stepping stones. She saw the path immediately, then the deer, a bounding blur of white.

She hurried after, taking each twist and turn of the path at a run. But always the deer stayed just ahead, with no more than a quick glimpse of gleaming white, and the thunder of hooves on the packed ground.

Then she was in a clearing. It seemed to open up out of nowhere, a perfect circle of soft earth ringed by majestic trees. And within the circle, another circle, made of dark gray stones, the shortest as high as her shoulder, the tallest just over her head.

Stunned, she reached out, touched her fingertips to the surface of the nearest stone. And would have sworn she felt a vibration, like harp strings being plucked. And heard in some secret part of her mind, the answering note.

A stone dance in Oregon? That was...certainly improbable, she decided. Yet here it was. It didn't strike her as being new, but surely it couldn't be otherwise. If it was ancient, someone would have written about it, tourists would come to see it, scientists to study.

Curious, she started to step through two stones, then immediately stepped back again. It seemed the air within quivered. The light was different—richer, and the sound of the sea closer than it had seemed only a moment before.

She told herself she was a rational woman, that there was no life in stone, nor any difference between the air where she stood and that one foot inside the circle. But rational or not, she skirted around rather than walking through.

It was as if the deer had waited, halfway around the dance just down a thin, shadowy path through the trees. Just as it seemed she looked at Rowan with understanding, and amusement before she bounded gracefully ahead.

This time when she followed, Rowan lost all sense of direction. She could hear the sea, but was it ahead, to the left, or to the right? The path twisted, turned and narrowed until it was no more than a track. She climbed over a fallen log, skidded down an incline and wandered through shadows deep as twilight.

When the path ended abruptly, leaving her surrounded by trees and thick brush, she cursed herself for an idiot. She turned, intending to retrace her steps, and saw that the track veered off in two directions.

For the life of her she couldn't remember which to take.

Then she saw the flash of white again, just a glimmer to the left. Heaving a breath, then holding it, Rowan pushed through the brush, fought her way out of the grasp of a thick, thorny vine. She slipped, righted herself. Cursing vividly now, she tripped and stumbled clear of the trees.

The cabin stood nearly on the cliffs, ringed by trees on three sides and backed by the rocks on the fourth. Smoke billowed from the chimney and was whisked away to nothing in the wind.

She pushed the hair out of her face, smeared a tiny drop of blood from a nick a thorn had given her. It was smaller than Belinda's cabin, and made of stone rather than wood. Sunlight had the mica glittering like diamonds. The porch was wide, but uncovered. On the second floor a small and charming stone balcony jutted out from glass doors.

When she lowered her gaze from it, Liam was standing on the porch. He had his thumbs hooked in the front pockets of his jeans, a black sweatshirt with its arms shoved up to the elbows. And he didn't look particularly happy to see her.

But he nodded. "Come in, Rowan. Have some tea."

He walked back inside without waiting for her response, and left the door open wide behind him. When she came closer, she heard the music, pipes and strings tangled in a weepy melody. She barely stopped her hands from twisting together as she stepped inside.

The living area seemed larger than she'd expected, but thought it was because the furnishings were very spare. A single wide chair, a long sofa, both in warm rust colors. A fire blazed under a mantel of dull gray slate. Gracing it was a jagged green stone as big as a man's fist and a statue of a woman carved in alabaster with her arms uplifted, her head thrown back, her naked body slender as a wand.

She wanted to move closer, to study the face, but it seemed rude. Instead she walked toward the back and found Liam in a small, tidy kitchen with a kettle already on the boil and lovely china cups of sunny yellow set out.

"I wasn't sure I'd find you," she began, then lost the rest of her thought as he turned from the stove, as those intense eyes locked on hers.

"Weren't you?"

"No, I hoped I would, but...I wasn't sure." Nerves reared up and grabbed her by the throat. "I made some cookies. I brought you some to thank you for helping me out last night."

He smiled a little and poured boiling water into a yellow pot. "What kind?" he asked. Though he knew. He'd smelled them, and her before she'd stepped out of the woods.

"Chocolate chip." She managed a smile of her own. "Is there another kind?" She busied her hands by opening the container. "They're pretty good. I've eaten two dozen at least already."

"Then sit. You can wash them back with tea. You'll have gotten chilled wandering about. The wind's brisk today."

"I suppose." She sat at the little kitchen table, just big enough for two. "I don't even know how long I've been out," she began, shoving at her tangled hair as he brought the pot to the table. "I was distracted by—" She broke off as he skimmed his thumb over her cheek.

"You've scratched your face." He said it softly as the tiny drop of blood lay warm and intimate on his thumb.

"Oh, I...got tangled up. Some thorns." She was lost in his eyes, could have drown in them. Wanted to. "Liam."

He touched her face again, took away the sting she was too befuddled to notice. "You were distracted," he said, shifting back, then sitting across from her. "When you were in the forest."

"Ah...yes. By the white doe."

He lifted a brow as he poured out the tea. "A white deer? Were you on a quest, Rowan?"

She smiled self-consciously. "The white deer, or bird, or horse. The traditional symbol of quest in literature. I suppose I was on a mild sort of quest, to find you. But I did see her."

"I don't doubt it," he said mildly. His mother enjoyed traditional symbols.

"Have you?"

"Yes." He lifted his tea. "Though it's been some time."

"She's beautiful, isn't she?"

"Aye, that she is. Warm yourself, Rowan. You've bird bones and you'll take a chill."

"I grew up in San Francisco. I'm used to chills.

Anyway, I saw her, and couldn't stop myself from following her. I ended up in this clearing, with a stone circle.''

His eyes sharpened, glinted. ''She led you there?''

''I suppose you could put it that way. You know the place? I never expected to find something like it here. You think of Ireland or Britain, Wales or Cornwall—not Oregon—when you think of stone dances.''

''You find them where they're wanted. Or needed. Did you go in?''

''No. It's silly, but it spooked me a little, so I went around. And got completely lost.''

He knew he should have felt relieved, but instead there was a vague sense of disappointment. But of course, he reminded himself, he'd have known if she'd stepped inside. Instantly. ''Hardly lost since you're here.''

''It seemed like I was lost. The path disappeared and I couldn't get my sense of direction. I probably have a poor one anyway. The tea's wonderful,'' she commented. It was warm and strong and smooth, with something lovely and sweet just under it.

''An old family blend,'' he said with a hint of a smile, then sampled one of her cookies. ''They're good. So you cook, do you, Rowan?''

''I do, but the results are hit and miss.'' All of her early-morning cheer was back and bubbling in her voice. ''This morning, I hit. I like your house. It's like something out of a book, standing here with its back to the cliffs and sea and the stones glittering in the sunlight.''

"It does for me. For now."

"And the views…" She rose to go to the window over the sink, and caught her breath at the sight of the cliffs. "Spectacular. It must be spellbinding during a storm like the one we had last night."

Spellbinding, he thought, knowing his father's habit of manipulating the weather for his needs, was exactly what the storm had been. "And did you sleep well?"

She felt the heat rise up her throat. She could hardly tell him she'd dreamed he'd made love to her. "I don't remember ever sleeping better."

He laughed, rose. "It's flattering." He watched her shoulders draw in. "To know my company relaxed you."

"Hmm." Struggling to shake off the feeling that he knew exactly where her mind had wandered, she started to turn. She noticed the open door and the little room beyond where he'd left a light burning on a desk, and a sleek black computer running.

"Is that your office?"

"In a manner of speaking."

"I've interrupted your work, then."

"It's not pressing." He shook his head. "Why don't you ask if you want to see?"

"I do," she admitted. "If it's all right."

In answer he simply gestured and waited for her to step into the room ahead of him.

The room was small, but the window was wide enough to let in that stunning view of the cliffs. She wondered how anyone could concentrate on work with that to dream on. Then laughed when she saw what was on the monitor screen.

"So you were playing games? I know this one. My students were wild for it. 'The Secrets Of Myor.'"

"Don't you play games?"

"I'm terrible at them. Especially this kind because I tend to get wrapped up in them, and then every step is so vital. I can't take the pressure." Laughing again, she leaned closer, studying the screen with its lightning-stalked castle and glowing faeries. "I've only gotten to the third level where Brinda the witch queen promises to open the Door Of Enchantment if you can find the three stones. I usually find one, then fall into The Pit Of Forever."

"There are always traps on the way to enchantment. Or there wouldn't be pleasure in finding it. Do you want to try again?"

"No, my palms get damp and my fingers fumble. It's humiliating."

"Some games you take seriously, some you don't."

"They're all serious to me." She glanced at the CD jacket, admiring the illustration, then blinked at the small lettering: Copyright By The Donovan Legacy. "It's your game?" Delighted, she straightened, turned. "You create computer games? That's so clever."

"It's entertaining."

"To someone who's barely stumbled their way onto the internet, it's genius. Myor's a wonderful story. The graphics are gorgeous, but I really admire the story itself. It's just magical. A challenging fairy tale with rewards and consequences.''

Her eyes took on tiny silver flecks of light when she was happy, he noted. And the scent of her warmed with her mood. He knew how to make it warm still more, and how to cause those silver flecks to drown in deep, dark blue.

''All fairy tales have both. I like your hair this way.'' He stepped closer, skimmed his fingers through it, testing weight and texture. ''Tumbled and tangled.''

Her throat snapped closed. ''I forgot to braid it this morning.''

''The wind's had it,'' he murmured, lifting a handful to his face. ''I can smell the wind on it, and the sea.'' It was reckless, he knew, but he had dreamed as well. And he remembered every rise and fall. ''I'd taste both on your skin.''

Her knees had jellied. The blood was swimming so fast in her veins that she could hear the roar of it in her head. She couldn't move, could barely breathe. So only stood, staring into his eyes, waiting.

''Rowan Murray with the faerie eyes. Do you want me to touch you.'' He laid a hand on her heart, felt each separate hammer blow pound between the gentle curves of her breasts. ''Like this.'' Then spread his fingers, circled them over one slope, under.

Her bones dissolved, her eyes clouded, and the breath shuddered between her lips in a yielding sigh. His fingers lay lightly on her, but the heat from them seemed to scorch through to flesh. Still she moved neither toward him nor away.

"You've only to say no," he murmured. "When I ask if you want me to taste you."

But her head fell back, those clouded eyes closed when he lowered his head to graze his teeth along her jawline. "The sea and the wind, and innocence as well." His own needs thickened his voice, but there was an edge on it. "Will you give me that as well, do nothing to stop me taking it?" He eased back, waiting, willing her eyes to open and look into his. "If I kissed you now, Rowan, what might happen?"

Her lips trembled apart as memory of a question once asked in dreams and never answered struggled to surface. Then his mouth was on hers, and every thought willingly died. Lights, a wild swirl of them behind the eyes. Heat, a hot gush of it in the belly. The first sound she made was a whimper that might have been fear, but the next was a moan that was unmistakably pleasure.

He was more gentle than she'd expected, perhaps more than he'd intended. His lips skimmed, sipped, nipped and nuzzled until hers went pillow soft and warm under them. She swayed against him in surrender, and request.

Oh, yes, I want this. Just this.

A shiver coursed through her as his hand circled the back of her neck, as he urged her head back, took the kiss deeper with a tangle of tongues and tastes, a mingle of breath that grew unsteady and quick. She gripped his shoulders, first for balance, then for the sheer joy of feeling that hard, dangerous strength, the bunch of muscles.

Her hands slid over and into his hair.

She had a flash of the wolf, the rich black pelt and sinewy strength, then of the man, sitting on her bed, gripping her hand as her body shuddered.

The memory of what could be in dreams, the barrage of sensations of what was, battered each other.

And she erupted.

Her mouth went wild under his, tore at his control. Her surrender had been sweet, but her demands were staggering. As his blood leaped he dragged her closer, let the kiss fly from warm, to hungry to something almost savage.

Still she urged him on, pulling him with her until he buried his face in her throat and had to fight not to use his teeth.

"You're not ready for me." He managed to pant it out, then yanked her back, shook her lightly. "By Finn, I'm not ready for you. There might come a time when that won't matter, and we'll take our chances. But it matters now." His grip lightened, his tone gentled. "It matters today. Go home, Rowan, where you'll be safe."

Her head was still spinning, her pulse still roaring. "No one's ever made me feel like that. I never knew anyone could."

Something flashed into his eyes that made her shiver in anticipation. But then he muttered in a language she didn't understand and lowered his brow to hers. "Honesty can be dangerous. I'm not always civilized, Rowan, but I work to be fair. Have a care how much you offer, for I'm likely to take more."

"I'm terrible at lying."

It made him laugh, and his eyes were calm again

when he straightened. "Then be quiet, for God's sake. Go home now. Not the way you came. You'll see the path when you head out the front. Follow it and you'll get home right enough."

"Liam, I want—"

"I know what you want." Firmly now he took her by the arm and led her out. "If it were as simple as going upstairs and rolling around on the bed for an afternoon, we'd already be there." While she sputtered, he continued to pull her to the front door. "But you're not as simple as you've been taught to think. God knows I'm not. Go on home with you, Rowan."

He all but shoved her out the door. Her rare and occasionally awesome temper shot to the surface as the wind slapped her face. "All right, Liam, because I don't want it to be simple." Her eyes flared at him as she dragged her hair back. "I'm tired of settling for simple. So don't put your hands on me again unless you mean to complicate things."

Riding on anger, she spun around, and didn't question the fact that the path was there, wide and clear. She just marched to it and strode into the trees.

From the porch he watched; long after she was out of sight, he continued to watch her, smiling a bit when she finally reached her own home and slammed the door behind her.

"Good for you, Rowan Murray."

Chapter 4

The man had thrown her out of his house, Rowan thought as she stormed into her own. One minute he'd been kissing her brainless, holding her against that marvelously male body—and the next he'd marched her to the door. Given her the boot as if she'd been some pesky saleswoman hawking an inferior product.

Oh, it was mortifying.

With temper still ringing in her ears like bells she strode around the living room, circled it twice. He'd put his hands on her, he'd made the moves. *He'd* kissed her, damn it. She hadn't done anything.

Except stand there like a dolt, she realized as temper sagged miserably into embarrassment. She'd just stood there, she thought as she wandered into the kitchen. And let him put his hands on her, let him kiss her. She'd have let him do anything, that was how dazzled she'd been.

"Oh, you're such a fool, Rowan." She dropped into a chair, and leaning over, lightly beat her head against the kitchen table. "Such a jerk, such a wimp."

She'd gone to him, hadn't she? Stumbling around in the woods like Gretel with a bunch of cookies instead of bread crumbs. Looking for magic, she thought and rested her cheek on the smooth wood. Always looking for something wonderful, she acknowledged with a sigh. And this time, for just a moment, she'd found it.

It was worse, she realized, when you had that staggering glimpse, then had the door slammed in your face.

God, was she so needy that she'd fall at the feet of a man she'd only met twice before, knew next to nothing about? Was she so weak and wobbly that she'd built fantasies around him because he had a beautiful face?

Not just his face, she admitted. It was the…essence of him, she supposed. The mystery, the romance of him that had very simply bewitched her. There was no other word that fit what he made her feel.

Obviously, quite obviously, it showed.

And when he had touched her because he'd seen through her pitiful ploy of seeking him out to thank him, she'd climbed all over him.

No wonder he'd shown her the door.

But he hadn't had to be so cruel about it, she thought, shoving up again. He'd humiliated her.

"You're not ready for me," she muttered, remembering what he'd said. "How the hell does he know

what I'm ready for when I don't know myself? He's
not a damn mind reader.''

Sulking now, she ripped the top off the container
of cookies and snatched one. She ate it with a scowl
on her face as she replayed that last scene, and gave
herself wonderful, pithy lines to put Liam Donovan
in his place.

''So, he didn't want me,'' she muttered. ''Who expected him to? I'll just stay out of his way. Completely. Totally.'' She shoved another cookie into her
mouth. ''I came here to figure out myself, not to try
to understand some Irish recluse.''

Slightly ill from the cookies, she snapped the lid
back on. The first thing she was going to do was drive
into town and find a bookstore. She was going to buy
some how-to books. Basic home maintenance, she decided, stalking back into the living room for her
purse.

She wasn't going to go fumbling around the next
time something happened. She'd figure out how to fix
it herself. And, she thought darkly as she marched out
of the house, if Liam came to her door offering to fix
it for her, she'd coolly tell him she could take care
of herself.

She slammed the door of the Rover, gunned the
engine. An errant thought about flat tires made her
think she'd better find a book on car repair while she
was at it.

She bumped along the dirt road, clamping down on
the urge to work off some of her frustration by stomp-
ing on the gas. Just where Belinda's little lane met
the main road, she saw the silver bird.

He was huge, magnificent. An eagle, she thought automatically stepping on the brake to stop and study him. Though she didn't know if any type of eagle was that regal silvery-gray or if they tended to perch on road signs to stare—balefully, she decided—at passing cars.

What wonderfully odd fauna they had in Oregon, she mused and reminded herself to read the books on local wildlife she'd brought with her more carefully. Unable to resist, she rolled down the window and leaned out.

"You're so handsome." She smiled as the bird ruffled his feathers and seemed to preen. "So regal. I bet you look magnificent in the air. I wonder what it feels like to fly. To just…own the sky. You'd know."

His eyes were green, she realized. A silver-gray eagle with eyes green as a cat's. For an instant, she thought she saw a glint of gold resting in his breast feathers, as if he wore a pendant. Just a trick of the light, she decided and with some regret leaned back in the window.

"Wolves and deer and eagles. Why would anybody live in the city? Bye, your highness."

When the Rover was out of sight, the eagle spread its wings, rose majestically into the sky with a triumphant call that echoed over hill and forest and sea. He soared over the trees, circled, then dived. White smoke swirled, the light shimmered, blue as a lightning flash.

And he touched down on the forest floor softly, on two booted feet.

He stood just over six feet, with a mane of silver

hair, eyes of glass green and a face so sharply defined it might have been carved from the marble found in the dark Irish hills. A burnished gold chain hung around his neck, and dangling from it was the amulet of his rank.

"Runs like a rabbit," he muttered. "Then blames herself for the fox."

"She's young, Finn." The woman who stepped out of the green shadows was lovely, with gilded hair flowing down her back, soft tawny eyes, skin white and smooth as alabaster. "And she doesn't know what's inside her, or understand what's inside of Liam."

"A backbone's what she's needing, a bit more of that spirit she showed when she spat in his eye not long ago." His fierce face gentled with a smile. "Never was a lack of spine or spirit a problem of yours, Arianna."

She laughed and cupped her husband's face in her hands. The gold ring of their marriage gleamed on one hand, and the fire of a ruby sparked on the other. "I've needed both with the likes of you, *a stor.* They're on their path, Finn. Now we must let them follow it in their own way."

"And who was it who led the girl to the dance, then to the lad?" he asked with an arrogantly raised eyebrow.

"Well then." Lightly, she trained a fingertip down his cheek. "I never said we couldn't give them a bit of a nudge, now and then. The lass is troubled, and Liam—oh, he's a difficult man, is Liam. Like his Da."

"Takes after his mother more." Still smiling, Finn leaned down to kiss his wife. "When the girl comes into her own, the boy will have his hands full. He'll be humbled before he finds the truth of pride. She'll be hurt before she finds the full of her strength."

"Then, if it's meant, they'll find each other. You like her." Arianna linked her hands at the back of Finn's neck. "She appealed to your vanity, sighing over you, calling you handsome."

His silver brows rose again, his grin flashed bright. "I am handsome—and so you've said yourself. We'll leave them to themselves a bit." He slid his arms around her waist. "Let's be home, *a ghra.* I'm already missing Ireland."

With a swirl of white smoke, a shiver of white light, they were home.

By the time Rowan got home, heated up a can of soup and devoured a section on basic plumbing repairs, it was sunset. For the first time since her arrival she didn't stop and stare and wonder at the glorious fire of the dying day. As the light dimmed, she merely leaned closer to the page.

With her elbows propped on the kitchen table, and her tea going cold, she almost wished a pipe would spring a leak so she could test out her new knowledge.

She felt smug and prepared, and decided to tackle the section on electrical work next. But first she'd make the phone call she'd been putting off. She considered fortifying herself with a glass of wine first, but decided that would be weak.

She took off her reading glasses, set them aside.
Slipped a bookmark into the pages, closed the book.
And stared at the phone.

It was terrible to dread calling people you loved.

She put it off just a little longer by neatly stacking
the books she'd bought. There were more than a
dozen, and she was still amused at herself for picking
up several on myths and legends.

They'd be entertaining, she thought, and wasted a
little more time selecting the one she wanted for bed-
time reading.

Then there was wood to be brought in for the evening fire, the soup bowl to wash and carefully dry.
Her nightly scan of the woods for the wolf she hadn't
seen all day.

When she couldn't find anything else to engage her
time, she picked up the phone and dialed.

Twenty minutes later, she was sitting on the back
steps, the backwash of light from the kitchen spilling
over her. And she was weeping.

She'd nearly buckled under the benign pressure,
nearly crumbled beneath the puzzled, injured tone of
her mother's voice. Yes, yes, of course, she'd come
home. She'd go back to teaching, get her doctorate,
marry Alan, start a family. She'd live in a pretty
house in a safe neighborhood. She'd be anything they
wanted her to be as long as it made them happy.

Not saying all of those things, not doing them was
so hard. And so necessary.

Her tears were hot and from the heart. She wished
she understood why she was always, always pulled in

a different direction, why she needed so desperately to see what was blurred at the edges of her mind.

Something was there, waiting for her. Something she was or needed to be. It was all she was sure of.

When the wolf nudged his head under her hand, she simply wrapped her arms around him and pressed her face to his throat.

"Oh, I hate hurting anyone. I can't bear it, and I can't stop it. What's wrong with me?"

Her tears dampened his neck. And touched his heart. To comfort he nuzzled her cheek, let her cling. Then he slipped a quiet thought into her mind.

Betray yourself, and you betray all they've given you. Love opens doors. It doesn't close them. When you go through it and find yourself, they'll still be there.

She let out a shuddering breath, rubbed her face against his fur. "I can't go back, even though part of me wants to. If I did, I know something inside me would just...stop." She leaned back, holding his head in her hands. "If I went back, I'd never find anything like you again. Even if it were there, I wouldn't really see it. I'd never follow a white doe or talk to an eagle."

Sighing, she stroked his head, his powerful shoulders. "I'd never let some gorgeous Irishman with a bad attitude kiss me, or do something as fun and foolish as eat cookies for breakfast."

Comforted, she rested her head against his. "I need to do those things, to be the kind of person who does them. That's what they can't understand, you know?

And it hurts and frightens them because they love me.''

She sighed again, leaned back, stroking his head absently as she studied the woods with their deep shadows, their whispering secrets. "So I have to make this all work, so they stop being hurt and stop being frightened. Part of me is scared that I will make it work—and part of me is scared I won't." Her lips curved ruefully. "I'm such a coward."

His eyes narrowed, glinted, a low growl sounded in his throat making her blink. Their faces were close, and she could see those strong, deadly white teeth. Swallowing hard, she stroked his head with fingers that trembled.

"There now. Easy. Are you hungry? I have cookies." Heart hammering, she got slowly to her feet as he continued to growl. She kept her eyes on him, walking backward as he came up the steps toward her.

As she reached the door, one part of her mind screamed for her to slam it, lock it. He was a wild thing, feral, not to be trusted. But with her eyes locked on his, all she could think was how he had pressed his muzzle against her, how he had been there when she wept.

She left the door open.

Though her hand shook, she picked up a cookie, held it out. "It's probably bad for you, but so many good things are." She muffled a yelp when he nipped it, with surprising delicacy, from her fingertips.

She'd have sworn his eyes laughed at her.

"Well okay, now we know sugar's as good as music for soothing savage beasts. One more, but that's it.''

When he rose onto his hind legs with surprising speed and grace, set those magnificent front paws on her shoulders, she could only manage a choked gasp. Her eyes, wide and round and shocked, met his glinting ones. Then he licked her, from collarbone to ear, one long, warm stroke, and made her laugh.

''What a pair we are,'' she murmured and pressed her lips to the ruff of his neck. ''What a pair.''

He lowered, just as gracefully, snatching the cookie from her fingers on the way.

''Clever, very clever.'' Eyeing him, she closed the lid on the cookies and set them on top of the refrigerator. ''What I need is a hot bath and a book,'' she decided. ''And that glass of wine I didn't let myself have before. I'm not going to think about what someone else wants,'' she continued as she turned to open the refrigerator. ''I'm not going to think about sexy neighbors with outrageously wonderful mouths. I'm going to think about how lovely it is to have all this time, all this space.''

She finished pouring the wine and lifted her glass in toast as he watched her. ''And to have you. Why don't you come upstairs and keep me company while I have that bath?''

The wolf ran his tongue around his teeth, let out a low sound that resembled a laugh and thought, *why don't I?*

She fascinated him. It wasn't a terribly comfortable sensation, but he couldn't shake it. It didn't matter how often he reminded himself she was an ordinary woman, and one with entirely too much baggage to become involved with.

He just couldn't stay away.

He'd been certain he'd tuned her out when she'd slammed her door behind her. Even though he'd been delighted with that flare of temper, the way it had flashed in her eyes, firmed that lovely soft mouth, he'd wanted to put her out of his mind for a few days.

Smarter, safer that way.

But he'd heard her weeping. Sitting in his little office, toying with a spin-off game for Myor, he'd heard those sounds of heartbreak, and despite the block he'd imposed, had felt her guilt and grief ripping at his heart.

He hadn't been able to ignore it. So he'd gone to her, offered a little comfort. Then she'd infuriated him, absolutely infuriated him by calling herself a coward. By believing it.

And what had the coward done, he thought, when a rogue wolf had snarled at her? Offered him a cookie.

A cookie, for Finn's sake.

She was utterly charming.

Then he had entertained, and tortured himself, by sitting and watching her lazily undress. Sweet God the woman had a way of sliding out of her clothes that made a man's head spin. Then, in a red robe she hadn't bothered to belt, she'd filled the old-fashioned tub with frothy bubbles that smelled of jasmine.

She'd lighted candles. Such a…female thing to do. She ran the water too hot, and had turned music on seductively low. As she shrugged out of the robe, she daydreamed. He resisted sliding into her mind to see what put that faraway look in her eyes, that faint smile on her lips.

Her body delighted him. It was so slender, so smooth, with a pearly sheen to the skin and slim, subtle curves. Delicate bones, tiny feet, and breasts tipped fragile blush-pink.

He wanted to taste there, to run his tongue from white to pink to white.

When she'd leaned over to turn off the taps, it had taken an enormous act of will to prevent himself from nipping at that firm, naked bottom.

It both irritated and charmed him that she seemed to have no vanity, no self-awareness. She piled her hair on top of her head in a gloriously messy mass, and didn't so much as glance at herself in the mirror.

Instead she talked to him, chattering nonsense, then hissed out a breath as she stepped into the tub. Steam billowed as she gingerly lowered herself, until the bubbles played prettily over her breasts.

Until he longed to reform and slip into the tub with her as a man.

She only laughed when he walked forward to sniff at her. Only ran a hand over his head absently while she picked up a book with the other.

Home Maintenance for the Confused and Inept.

It made him chuckle, the sound coming out as a soft *woof*. She gave his ears a quick scratch, then reached for her wine.

"It says here," she began, "that I should always have a few basic tools on hand. I think I saw all of these in the utility room, but I'd better make a list and compare. The next time the power goes out, or I blow a fuse—or is it a breaker?—I'm handling it myself. I won't be rescued by anyone, especially Liam Donovan.''

She gasped then chuckled when the wolf dipped his tongue into her glass and drank. ''Hey, hey! This is a very fine sauvignon blanc, and not for you, pal.'' She lifted the glass out of reach. ''It explains how to do simple rewiring,'' she continued. ''Not that I'm planning on doing any, but it doesn't look terribly complicated. I'm very good at following directions.''

A frown marred her brow. ''Entirely too good.'' She sipped wine, slid lower in the tub. ''That's the core of the problem. I'm *used* to following directions, so everyone's startled that I've taken a detour.''

She set the book aside, idly lifted a leg out of the water, skimmed a fingertip up her calf.

His mind moaned.

''No one's more surprised than I am that I like detours. Adventures,'' she added and grinned over at him. ''This is really my first adventure.'' She eased up again, bubbles clinging to her breasts. She scooped up a handful and idly rubbed them up and down her arm.

She only laughed when he ran his tongue slowly from her elbow to her shoulder. ''All in all, it's been a hell of an adventure so far.''

She lingered in the tub for a half hour, innocently delighting him. The scent of her as she toweled off made him yearn. He found her no less alluring when she slipped into the flannel pajamas.

When she crouched to build up the bedroom fire, he nipped and nuzzled, making her giggle. The next thing she knew she was wrestling playfully with a wolf on the hearth rug. His breath tickled her throat. She rubbed his belly and made him rumble with pleasure. His tongue was warm and wet on her cheek. Breathlessly happy she knelt to throw her arms around his neck, to hug fiercely.

"Oh, I'm so glad you're here. I'm so glad I found you." She pressed her cheek hard against his, locked her fingers in that silky fur. "Or did you find me?" she murmured. "It doesn't matter. It's so good to have a friend who doesn't expect anything but friendship."

She curled up with him to watch the fire, smiling at the pictures she found in the flames. "I've always liked doing this. When I was a little girl I was sure I saw things in the fire. Magic things," she murmured, and settled her head on his neck. "Beautiful things. Castles and clouds and cliffs." Her voice slurred as her eyes grew heavy. "Handsome princes and enchanted hills. I used to think I could go there, through the smoke and into the magic." She sighed, drifted. "Now there are only shapes and light."

And slept.

When she slept, he let himself be Liam, stroking her hair while he watched the fire she'd built. There was a way through the smoke and into the magic, he thought. What would she think if he showed her? If he took her there?

"But you'd have to come back to the other, Rowan. There's no way for me to keep you. I don't want to keep you," he corrected, firmly. "But God, I want to have you."

In sleep she sighed, shifted. Her arm came around him. He closed his eyes. "You'd best hurry," he told her. "Hurry and find out what you want and where you intend to go. Sooner or later I'll send for you."

He rose, lifting her gently to carry her to bed. "If you come to me," he whispered as he lowered her to the bed, spread the cover over her. "If you come to me, Rowan Murray, I'll show you magic." Lightly he touched his lips to hers. "Dream what you will tonight, and dream alone."

He kissed her again, for himself this time. He left her as a man. And prowled the night mists as a wolf.

She spent the next week in the grip of tremendous energy, compelled to fill every minute of every day with something new. She explored the woods, haunted the cliffs and pleased herself by sketching whatever appealed to the eye.

As the weather gradually warmed, the bulbs she'd spotted began to bud. The night still carried a chill, but spring was ready to reign. Delighted, she left the windows open to welcome it in.

For that week she saw no one but the wolf. It was rare for him not to spend at least an hour with her. Walking with her on her hikes through the woods, waiting patiently while she examined the beginnings of a wildflower, a circle of toadstools or stopped to sketch the trees.

Her weekly call home made her heart ache, but she

told herself she felt strong. Dutifully she wrote a long letter to Alan, but said nothing about coming back.

Each morning she woke content. Each night she slipped into bed satisfied. Her only frustration was that she'd yet to discover what she needed to do. Unless, she sometimes thought, what she needed was simply to live alone with her books, her drawings and the wolf.

She hoped there was more.

Liam did not wake every morning content. Nor did he go to bed every night satisfied. He blamed her for it, though he knew it was unfair.

Still if she'd been less innocent, he would have taken what she'd once offered him. The physical need would have been met. And he assured himself this emotional pull would fade.

He refused to accept whatever fate had in store for him, for them, until he was completely in control of his own mind and body.

He stood facing the sea on a clear afternoon when the wind was warm and the air full of rioting spring. He'd come out to clear his head. His work wouldn't quite gel. And though he claimed continually that it was no more than a diversion, an amusement, he took a great deal of pride in the stories he created.

Absently he fingered the small crystal of fluorite he'd slipped into his pocket. It should have calmed him, helped to steady his mind. Instead his mind was as restless as the sea he studied.

He could feel the impatience in the air, mostly his own. But he knew the sense of waiting was from others. Whatever destination he was meant to reach, the steps to it were his own. Those who waited asked when he would take them.

"When I'm damned ready," he muttered. "My life remains mine. There's always a choice. Even with responsibility, even with fate, there is a choice. Liam, son of Finn, will make his own."

He wasn't surprised to see the white gull soar overhead. Her wing caught the sunlight, tipped gracefully as she flew down. And her eyes glinted, gold as his own, when she perched on a rock.

"Blessed be, Mother."

With only a bit more flourish than necessary, Arianna swirled from bird to woman. She smiled, opened her arms. "Blessed me, my love."

He went to her, enfolded her, pressed his face into her hair. "I've missed you. Oh, you smell of home."

"Where you, too, are missed." She eased back, but framed his face in her hands. "You look tired. You aren't sleeping well."

Now his smile was rueful. "No, not well. Do you expect me to?"

"No." And she laughed, kissed both his cheeks before turning to look out to sea. "This place you've chosen to spend some time is beautiful. You've always chosen well, Liam, and you will always have a choice." She slanted a look up at him. "The woman is lovely, and pure of heart."

"Did you send her to me?"

"The one day? Yes, or I showed her the way." Arianna shrugged and walked back to sit on the rock. "But did I send her here, no. There are powers beyond mine and yours that set events in order. You know that.'' She crossed her legs and the long white dress she wore whispered. ''You find her attractive.''

''Why wouldn't I?''

''She's not the usual type you're drawn to, at least to dally with.''

He set his teeth. ''A grown man doesn't care to have his mother discuss his sex life.''

''Oh.'' She waved a hand dismissively and set her rings flashing. ''Sex, when tempered with respect and affection, is healthy. I want my only child to be healthy, don't I? You won't dally with her because you worry it will involve more than sex, more than affection.''

''And what then?'' Anger simmered in his voice. ''Do I take her, engage her heart only to hurt her? 'An it harm none.' Does that only apply to magic?''

''No.'' She spoke gently, held out a hand to him. ''It should apply to life. Why assume you'll harm her, Liam?''

''I'm bound to.''

''No more than any man hurts any woman when their hearts bump together. You would take the same risks with her.'' She angled her head as she studied his face. ''Do you think your father and I have loved over thirty years without a scratch or bruise?''

''She's not like us.'' He squeezed the hand he held, then released it. ''If I take the steps, if I let us both feel more than we do now, I'd have to let her go or turn my back on my obligations. Obligations you know I came here to sort out.'' Furious with himself, he turned back to the sea. "I haven't even done that. I know my father wants me to take his place."

"Well not quite yet," Arianna said with a laugh. "But yes, when the time is right, it's hoped you'll stand as head of the family, as Liam of Donovan, to guide."

"It's a power I can pass to another. That's my right."

"Aye, Liam." Concerned now, she slid from the rock to go to him. "It's your right to step aside, to let another wear the amulet. Is that what you want?"

"I don't know." Frustration rang in his voice. "I'm not my father. I don't have his…way with others. His judgment. His patience or his compassion."

"No. You have your own." She laid a hand on his arm. "If you weren't fit for the responsibility, you would not be given it."

"I've thought of that, tried to come to accept it. And I know that if I commit to a woman not of elfin blood, I abdicate the right to take those responsibilities. If I let myself love her, I turn my back on my obligations to my family."

Arianna's eyes sharpened as she studied his face. "Would you?"

"If I let myself love her, I'd turn my back on anything, on everything but her."

She closed her eyes then, felt the tears welling in them. "Oh, it's proud I am to hear it, Liam." Eyes drenched she lay a hand on his heart. "There is no stronger magic, no truer power than love. This above all I want you to learn, to know, to feel."

Her hand closed into a fist so quickly, her eyes

flashed with annoyance so abruptly, he could only
gape when she rapped his chest. "And for the love
of Finn why haven't you looked? Your powers are
your gifts, your birthright and more acute than any I
know but your father. What have you been doing?"
she demanded, throwing up her hands and whirling
with a spin of white silk. "Prowling the woods, calling to the moon, spinning your games. And brooding," she added, jabbing a finger at him as she turned
back. "Oh, a champion brooder you ever were, and
that's the truth of it. You'll torture yourself with the
wanting of her, go keep her company during a
storm—"

"Which I know bloody well Da brewed."

"That's beside the point," she snapped and skew-
ered him with the sharp, daunting look he remembered from childhood. "If you don't spend time with
the girl you won't think with anything but your
glands, will you? The sex won't answer it all, you
horse's ass. It's just like a man to think it will."

"Well, damn it, I *am* a man."

"What you are is a pinhead, and don't you raise
your voice to me, Liam Donovan."

He threw up his hands as well, added a short, pithy
curse in Gaelic. "I'm not twelve any longer."

"I don't care if you're a hundred and twelve, you'll
show your mother proper respect."

He smoldered, seethed and sucked it in. "Yes,
ma'am."

"Aye." She nodded once. "That'll do. Now stop
tormenting yourself with what may be, and look at
what is. And if your lofty principles won't let you

look deep enough, ask her about her mother's family.''

Arianna let out a huff of breath, smoothed down her hair. ''And kiss me goodbye like a good lad. She'll be here any second.''

Because he was still scowling she kissed him instead, then grinned sunnily. ''There are times you look so like your Da. Now don't look so fierce, you'll frighten the girl. Blessed be, Liam,'' she added, then with a shiver of the light, spread white wings and soared into the sky.

Chapter 5

He hadn't sensed her, and that irritated him. His temper had been up, blocking his instincts. Now, even as he turned, he caught that scent—female, innocence with a light whiff of jasmine.

He watched her come out of the trees, though she didn't see him—not at first. The sun was behind him, and she looked the other way as she started up the rough path to the apex of the cliffs.

She had her hair tied back, he noted, in a careless tail of gleaming brown the wind caught and whipped. She carried a trim leather bag with its strap crosswise over her body. Her gray slacks showed some wear and her shirt was the color of daffodils.

Her mouth was unpainted, her nails short, her boots—so obviously new—showed a long, fresh scar across the left toe. The sight of her, muttering to herself as she climbed, both relaxed and annoyed him.

Then both sensations turned to pure amusement as she spotted him, jolted and scowled before she could school her expression to disinterest.

"Good morning to you, Rowan."

She nodded, then clasped both hands on the strap of her bag as if she didn't know what else to do with them. Her eyes were cool, in direct contrast to those nervous hands, and quite deliberately skimmed past him.

"Hello. I'd have gone another way if I'd known you were here. I imagine you want to be alone."

"Not particularly."

Her gaze veered back to his, then away again. "Well, I do," she said very definitely and began to make her way along the rocks away from him.

"Hold a grudge, do you, Rowan Murray?"

Stiffening with pride, she kept walking. "Apparently."

"You won't be able to for long, you know. It's not natural for you."

She jerked a shoulder, knowing the gesture was bad-tempered and childish. She'd come to sketch the sea, the little boats that bobbed on it, the birds that soared and called above. And damn it, she'd wanted to look at the eggs in the nest to see if they'd hatched.

She hadn't wanted to see him, to be reminded of what had happened between them, what it had stirred inside her. But neither was she going to be chased away like a mouse by a cat. Setting her teeth, she sat on a ledge of rock, opened her bag. With precise movements she pulled out her bottle of water, put it beside her, then her sketchbook, then a pencil.

Ordering herself to focus, she looked out at the water, gave herself time to scan and absorb. She began to sketch, telling herself she would not look over at him. Oh, he was still there, she was sure of it. Why else would every muscle in her body be on alert, why would her heart still be tripping in her chest?

But she would not look.

Of course she looked. And he was still there, a few paces away, his hands tucked casually in his pockets, his face turned toward the water. It was just bad luck, she supposed, that he was so attractive, that he could stand there with the wind in all that glorious hair, his profile sharp and clean, and remind her of Heathcliff or Byron or some other poetic hero.

A knight before battle, a prince surveying his realm.

Oh, yes, he could be any and all of them—as romantic in jeans and a sweatshirt as any warrior glinting in polished armor.

"I don't mean to do battle with you, Rowan."

She thought she heard him say it, but that was nonsense. He was too far away for those soft words to carry. She'd just imagined that's what he *would* say in response if she'd spoken her thoughts aloud. So she sniffed, glanced back down at her book and to her disgust noted that she'd begun to sketch him without realizing it.

With an irritated flick, she turned to a blank page.

"There's no point in being angry with me—or yourself."

This time she knew he'd spoken, and looked up to see that he'd strolled over to her. She had to squint, to shade her eyes with the flat of her hand as the sun streamed behind him and shimmered its light like a nimbus around his head and shoulders.

"There's no point in discussing it."

She huffed out a breath as he sat companionably beside her. When he lapsed into silence, appeared to be settling in for a nice long visit, she tapped her pencil on her pad.

"It's a long coast. Would you mind plopping down on another part of it?"

"I like it here." When she hissed and started to rise, he simply tugged her back down. "Don't be foolish."

"Don't tell me I'm foolish. I'm really, really tired of being told I'm foolish." She jerked her arm free. "And you don't even know me."

He shifted so they were face-to-face. "That could be part of it. What are you drawing there in your book?"

"Nothing apparently." Miffed, she stuffed the book back into her bag. Once again she started to rise. Once again he tugged her easily back.

"All right," she snapped. "We'll discuss it. I admit I stumbled my way through the woods because I wanted to see you. I was attracted—I'm sure you're used to women being attracted to you. I did want to thank you for your help, but that was only part of it. I intruded, no question, but you were the one who kissed me."

"I did indeed," he murmured. He wanted to do so again, right now when her mouth was in a stubborn pout and there was both distress and temper in her eyes.

"And I overreacted to it." The memory of that still made her blood heat. "You had a perfect right to tell me to go, but you didn't have the right to be so unkind about it. No one has the right to be unkind. Now, obviously, you didn't have the same…response I did and you want to keep your distance."

She pushed at the hair that was coming loose from her ponytail to fly in her face. "So why are you here?"

"Let's take this in order," he decided. "Yes, I'm used to women being attracted to me. As I've a fondness for women I appreciate that." A smile tugged at his lips as she made a quiet sound of disgust. "You'd think more of me if I lied about that, but I find false modesty inane and deceitful. And though I most often prefer to be alone, your visit wasn't intrusive. I kissed you because I wanted to, because you have a pretty mouth."

He watched it register surprise before it thinned and she angled her face away. No one's told her that before, he realized, and shook his head over the idiocy of the male gender.

"Because you have eyes that remind me of the elves that dance in the hills of my country. Hair like oak that's aged and polished to a gleam. And skin so soft it seems my hand should pass through it as it would with water."

"Don't do that." Her voice shook as she lifted her arms, wrapped them tight to hug her elbows. "Don't. It's not fair."

Perhaps it wasn't, to use words on a woman who so obviously wasn't used to hearing them. But he shrugged. "It's just truth. And my response to you was more...acute than I'd bargained for. So I was unkind. I apologize for that, Rowan, but only for that."

She was over her head with him, and wished the terror of that wasn't quite so enjoyable. "You're sorry for being unkind, or for having a response to me?"

Clever woman, he mused, and gave her the simple truth. "For both if it comes to it. I said I wasn't ready for you, Rowan. I meant it."

It was hearing simple truth that softened her heart—and made it tremble just a little. She didn't speak for a moment, but stared down at the fingers she'd locked together in her lap while waves crashed below and gulls soared overhead.

"Maybe I understand that, a little. I'm at an odd place in my life," she said slowly. "A kind of crossroads, I suppose. I think people are most vulnerable when they come to the end of something and have to decide which beginning they're going to take. I don't know you, Liam." She made herself shift back to face him again. "And I don't know what to say to you, or what to do."

Was there a man alive who could resist that kind of unstudied honesty? he wondered. "Offer me tea."

"What?"

He smiled, took her hand. "Offer me tea. Rain's coming and we should go in."

"Rain? But the sun's—" Even as she said it, the light changed. Dark clouds slipped through the sky without a sound and the first drops, soft as a wish, fell.

His father wasn't the only one who could use the weather for his own purposes.

"Oh, it was supposed to be clear all day." She stuffed the bottle of water back into her bag, then let out a quick gasp when he pulled her to her feet with casual, effortless strength that left her limbs oddly weak.

"It's just a shower, and a warm one at that." He began to guide her through the rocks, down the path. "Soft weather, we call it at home. Do you mind the rain?"

"No, I like it. It always makes me dreamy." She lifted her face, let a few drops kiss it. "The sun's still shining."

"You'll have a rainbow," he promised and tugged her into the sheltering trees where the air was warm and wet, and shadows lay in deep green pools. "Will I have tea?"

She slanted him a look, and a smile. "I suppose."

"There, I told you." He gave her hand a little squeeze. "You don't know how to hold a grudge."

"I just need practice," she said and made him laugh.

"I'm likely to give you plenty of cause for practice before we're done."

"Do you make a habit of annoying people?"

"Oh, aye. I'm a difficult man." They strolled by the stream where damp ferns and rich moss spread, and foxglove waited to bloom. "My mother says I'm a brooder, and my father that I've a head like a rock. They should know.''

"Are they in Ireland?"

"Mmm." He couldn't be sure unless he looked—and he damn well didn't want to know if they were lingering nearby watching him.

"Do you miss them?"

"I do, yes. But we…keep in touch." It was the wistfulness in her voice that had him glancing down as they walked into her clearing. "You're missing your family?"

"I'm feeling guilty because I don't miss them as much as I probably should. I've never been away alone before, and I'm—"

"Enjoying it," he finished.

"Enormously." She laughed a little and fished her keys out of her pocket.

"No shame in that." He cocked his head as she unlocked the door. "Who are you locking out?"

Her smile was a little sheepish as she stepped inside. "Habit. I'll put the tea on. I baked some cinnamon rolls earlier, but they're burned on the bottom. One of my misses."

"I'll take one off your hands." He wandered into the kitchen behind her.

She kept the room neat, he noted, and had added a few touches—the sort he recognized as a kind of nesting. Female making a home. Some pretty twigs speared out of one of Belinda's colorful bottles and stood in the center of the kitchen table beside a white bowl filled with bright green apples.

He remembered when she'd scouted out the twigs.

The wolf had walked with her—and had regally ignored her attempts to teach him to fetch.

He sat comfortably at her table, enjoying the quiet patter of rain. And thought of his mother's words. No, he wouldn't look that deeply. He didn't mind a skim through the thoughts, but that deliberate search was something he considered an abuse of power.

A man who demanded privacy had to respect that of others.

But he would pry without a qualm.

"Your family lives in San Francisco."

"Hmm. Yes." She had the kettle on and was choosing from one of Belinda's delightful collection of teapots. "They're both college professors. My father chairs the English department at the university."

"And your mother?" Idly, he slipped the sketchpad out of the bag she tossed on the table.

"She teaches history." After a mild debate, she selected a pot shaped like a faerie with wings for the handle. "They're brilliant," she continued, carefully measuring out tea. "And really marvelous instructors. My mother was made assistant dean last year and…"

She trailed off, stunned and just a little horrified when she saw Liam studying her sketch of the wolf.

"These are wonderful." He didn't bother to look up, but turned another page and narrowed his eyes in concentration at her drawing of a stand of trees and lacy ferns. Peeking through those airy shapes were the suggestion of wings, of laughing eyes.

She saw the faeries, he thought and smiled.

"They're just doodles." Her fingers itched to

snatch the book, close it away, but manners held her back. "It's just a hobby."

And when his eyes shot to hers, she nearly shivered.

"Why would you say that, and try to believe it, when you have a talent and a love for it?"

"It's only something I do in my spare time—now and again."

He turned the next page. She'd done a study of the cottage, made it look like something out of an old and charming legend with its ring of trees and welcoming porch. "And you're insulted when someone calls you foolish?" he muttered. "It's foolish you are if you don't do what you love instead of wringing your hands about it."

"That's a ridiculous thing to say. I do not wring my hands." She turned back to take the kettle off the bowl and prevent herself from doing exactly that. "It's a hobby. Most people have one."

"It's your gift," he corrected, "and you've been neglecting it."

"You can't make a living off of doodles."

"What does making a living have to do with it?"

His tone was so arrogantly royal, she had to laugh. "Oh, nothing other than food, shelter, responsibility." She came back to set the pot on the table, turned to fetch cups. "Little things like that from the real world."

"Then sell your art if you've a need to make a living."

"Nobody's going to buy pencil sketches from an English teacher."

"I'll buy this one." He rose and held the book open to one of her studies of the wolf. In it, the wolf stood, facing the onlooker with a challenging glint in his eyes exactly like the one in Liam's. "Name your price."

"I'm not selling it, and you're not buying it to make some point." Refusing to take him seriously, she waved him back. "Sit down and have your tea."

"Then give me the sketch." He angled his head as he looked at it again. "I like it. And this one." He flipped the page to the trees and fern faeries. "I could use something like this in the game I'm doing. I've no talent for drawing."

"Then who does the drawings for your graphics?" She asked hoping to change the subject, and as a last resort, got out the burned buns.

"Mmm. Different people for different moods." He sat again, absently took one of the rolls. It was hard and undeniably burned, but if you got past that, it was wonderfully sweet and generously filled with currants.

"So how do you—"

"Do either of your parents draw?" he interrupted.

"No." Even the thought of it made her chuckle. The idea of either of her smart and busy parents settling down to dream with pencil and paper. "They gave me lessons when I was a child and showed an interest. And my mother actually keeps a sketch I made of the bay when I was a teenager framed and in her office at the university."

"So she appreciates your talent."

"She loves her daughter," Rowan corrected and poured the tea.

"Then she should expect the daughter she loves to pursue her own gifts, explore her own talents," he said casually, but continued down the path of her family. "Perhaps one of your grandparents was an artist."

"No, my paternal grandfather was a teacher. It seems to come naturally through the family. My grandmother on that side was what I suppose you'd call a typical wife and mother of her time. She still keeps a lovely home."

He struggled against impatience—and against a wince as Rowan added three spoons of sugar to her cup. "And on your mother's side?"

"Oh, my grandfather's retired now. They live in San Diego. My grandmother does beautiful needlework, so I suppose that's a kind of art." Her lips pursed for a moment as she stirred her tea. "Now that I think of it, her mother—my great-grandmother painted. We have a couple of her oils. I think my grandmother and her brother have the rest. She was…eccentric," Rowan said with a grin.

"Was she now? And how was she eccentric?"

"I never knew her, but children pick up bits and pieces when adults gossip. She read palms and talked to animals—all decidedly against her husband's wishes. He was, as I recall, a very pragmatic Englishman, and she was a dreamy Irishwoman."

"So, she was Irish, was she?" Liam felt a low vibration along his spine. A warning, a frisson of power. "And her family name?"

"Ah…" Rowan searched back through her memory. "O'Meara. I'm named for her," she continued, contentedly drinking tea while everything inside Liam went on alert. "My mother named me for her in what she calls an irresistible flash of sentiment. I suppose that's why she—my great-grandmother—left me her pendant. It's a lovely old piece. An oval moonstone in a hammered silver setting."

In a slow and deliberate move, Liam set aside the tea he could no longer taste. "She was Rowan O'Meara."

"That's right. I think there was some wonderfully romantic story—or else I've made it up—about how my great-grandfather met her when he was on holiday in Ireland. She was painting on the cliffs—in Clare. That's odd, I don't know why I'm so sure it was Clare."

She puzzled over that for a moment, then shrugged it away. "Anyway, they fell in love on the spot, and she went back to England with him, left her home and her family. Then they immigrated to America, and eventually settled in San Francisco."

Rowan O'Meara from Clare. By the goddess, fate had twisted around and laid one more trap for him. He picked up his tea again to wet his throat. "My mother's family name is O'Meara." He spoke in a voice that was flat and cool. "Your great-grandmother would be a distant cousin of mine."

"You're kidding." Stunned and delighted, Rowan beamed at him.

"In matters such as family, I try not to joke."

"That would be amazing. Absolutely. Well, it's a small world." She laughed and lifted her cup. "Nice to meet you. Cousin Liam."

In the name of the goddess, he thought, and fatalistically tapped his cup to hers. The woman currently smiling at him out of those big, beautiful eyes had elfin blood, and didn't even know it.

"There's your rainbow, Rowan." He continued to look at her, but he knew the colored arch had spread in the sky outside. He hadn't conjured it—but sensed his father had.

"Oh!" She leaped up, and after one quick peek out the window, dashed to the door. "Come out and see. It's wonderful!"

She raced out, clattered down the steps and looked up.

She'd never seen one so clear, so perfectly defined. Against the watery-blue sky, each luminous layer stood out, shimmering at the edges with gold, melting into the next color, from rose to lavender to delicate yellow to candy-pink. It spread high, each tip grazing the tops of the trees.

"I've never seen one so beautiful."

When he joined her, he was both disconcerted and touched when she took his hand. But even as he looked up at the arch, he promised himself he wouldn't fall in love with her unless it was what he wanted.

He wouldn't be maneuvered, cajoled, seduced. He would make his decision with a clear mind.

But that didn't mean he couldn't take some of what he wanted in the meantime.

"This means nothing more, and nothing less than the other," he said.

"What?"

"This." He cupped her face, bent down and laid his lips on hers.

Soft as silk, gentle as the rain that was still falling through the pearly sunlight. He would keep it that way, for both of them, and lock down on the needs that were fiercer, more keen than was wise or safe.

Just a taste of that innocence, a glimpse of that tender heart she had no idea how to defend, he told himself. He would do what he could to keep that heart from falling too deeply or he might be forced to break it.

But when her hand came up to rest on his shoulder, when her mouth yielded so utterly under his, he felt those darker needs clawing for freedom.

She couldn't stop herself from giving, could hold nothing back against such tenderness. Even when the fingers on her face tightened, his mouth remained soft, easy, as if teaching hers what there was, what there could be.

Instinctively she soothed her hands over the tension of his shoulders and let herself sink into him.

He eased away before desire could outrace reason. When she only stared up at him with those exotic eyes blurred, those soft lips parted, he let her go.

"I guess it's just, ah, chemistry." Her heart was pounding in great, hammering leaps.

"Chemistry," he said, "can be dangerous."

"You can't make discoveries without some risks." It should have shocked her, a comment like that coming out of her mouth, such an obvious invitation to continue, to finish. But it seemed natural, and right.

"In this case it's best you know all the elements

you're dealing with. How much are you willing to find out, I wonder?''

"I came here to find out all sorts of things." She let out a quiet breath. "I didn't expect to find you."

"No. You're looking for Rowan first." He hooked his thumbs in his pockets, rocked back on his heels. "If I took you inside, took you here for that matter, you'd find a part of her quickly enough. Is that what you want?"

"No." It was another surprise to hear the denial when every nerve in her body was sizzling. "Because then it would be as you said before. Simple. I'm not looking for simple."

"Still, I'll kiss you again, when I've a mind to."

She angled her head, ignored the quick flutter in her belly. "I'll let you kiss me again, when *I've* a mind to."

He flashed a grin full of power and appreciation. "You've some of that Irishwoman in you, Rowan of the O'Mearas."

"Maybe I do." It pleased her enormously just then to think so. "Maybe I'll have to find more."

"That you will." His grin faded. "When you do, I hope you know what to do about it. Pick a day next week and come over. Bring your sketchbook."

"What for?"

"An idea I have brewing. We'll see if it suits both of us."

It couldn't hurt, she mused. And it would give her some time to think about everything that had happened that morning. "All right, but one day's the same as the next to me. My schedule's open these days.''

''You'll know which day when it comes.'' He reached out to toy with the ends of her hair. ''So will I.''

''And that, I suppose, is some kind of Irish mysticism.''

''You don't know the half of it,'' he murmured. ''A good day to you, Cousin Rowan.''

He gave her hair an absent tug, then turned and walked away.

Well, she thought, as days went, it hadn't been half-bad so far.

And when he came to her again in dreams, she welcomed him. When his mind touched hers, seduced it, aroused it, she sighed, yielded, offered.

She shivered in pleasure, breathed his name and sensed somehow that he was as vulnerable as she. For just that moment, just that misty space of time he was tangled with her, helpless not to give what she asked.

If only she knew the question.

Even when her body glowed, her mind soared, part of her fretted.

What should she ask him? What did she need to know?

In the dark, with the half-moon spilling delicate light through her open windows, she woke alone. She burrowed into the pillows and listened with her heart aching at the sound of the wolf calling to the night.

Chapter 6

Rowan watched spring burst into life. And watching, it seemed something burst into life inside her as well. Daffodils and windflowers shimmered into bloom. The little pear tree outside the kitchen window opened its delicate white blossoms and danced in the wind.

Deep in the forest, the wild azaleas began to show hints of pink and white, and the foxglove grew fat buds. There were others, so many others; she promised herself a book on local wildflowers on her next trip into town. She wanted to know them, learn their habits and their names.

All the while she felt herself begin to bloom. Was there more color in her face? she wondered, more light in her eyes? She knew she smiled more often, enjoyed the sensation of feeling her own lips curve up for no particular reason as she walked or sketched or simply sat on the porch in the warming air to read for hours.

Nights no longer seemed lonely. When the wolf came, she talked to him about whatever was on her mind. When he didn't, she was content to spend her evening alone.

She wasn't entirely sure what was different, only that something was. And that there were other, bigger changes yet to come.

Maybe it was the decision she'd made not to go back to San Francisco, or to teaching, or the practical apartment minutes from her parents' home.

She'd been cautious with money, she reminded herself. She'd never felt any particular urge to collect things or fill her closet with clothes or take elaborate vacations. Added to that was the small inheritance that had come down to her through her mother's family. One she had cautiously invested and watched grow neatly over the last few years.

There was enough to draw on for a down payment for a little house somewhere.

Somewhere quiet and beautiful, she thought now as she stood on the front porch with a cup of steaming coffee to welcome another morning. It had to be a house, she knew. No more apartment living. And somewhere in the country. She wasn't going to be happy in the bustle and rush of the city ever again. She'd have a garden she planted herself—once she learned how—and maybe a little creek or pond.

It had to be close enough to the sea that she could walk to it, hear its song at night as she drifted toward sleep.

Maybe, just maybe, on that next trip to town she'd visit a realtor. Just to see what was available.

It was such a big step—choosing a spot, buying a house—furnishing it, maintaining it. She caught herself winding the tip of her braid around her finger and deliberately dropped her hand. She was ready to make that step. She *would* make it.

And she'd find work, the kind that satisfied her. She didn't need a great deal of money. She'd be blissfully content puttering around some little cottage of her own, doing the painting, the repairs, watching her garden grow.

If she found something nearby, she wouldn't have to leave the wolf.

Or Liam.

With that thought, she shook her head. No, she couldn't add Liam into the equation, or make him part of the reason she was considering settling in the area. He was his own man, and would come and go when and where he pleased.

Just like the wolf, she realized and sighed. Neither one of them were hers, after all. They were both loners, both beautiful creatures who belonged to no one. And who'd come into her life—helped change it in some ways, she supposed. Though the biggest changes were up to her.

It seemed that after three weeks in the little cabin in the clearing, she was ready to make them. Not just drifting anymore, she thought. Not just wondering. Time to take definite steps.

The subtle tug at her mind had her eyes narrowing, her head angling as if to hear something soft whispered in the distance. It was almost as if she could hear her name, quietly called.

He'd said to come to him, she remembered. That she'd know when the time was right. Well, there was no time like the present, no better time than when she was in such a decisive mood. And after the visit, she'd drive into town and see that realtor.

He knew she was coming. He'd been careful to keep his contact with her limited over the past several days. Perhaps he hadn't been able to stay away completely. He did worry about her just a bit, thinking of her alone, and more out of her element than she knew.

But it was easy enough to check up on her, to walk to her door and have her open it for him. He could hardly deny he enjoyed the way she welcomed him, bending down to stroke his head and back or nuzzle her face against his throat.

She had no fear of the wolf, he mused. He only made her wary when he was a man.

But she was coming to the man, and would have to deal with him. He thought his plan a good one, for both of them. One that would give her the opportunity to explore her own talents—and would give each of them time to learn more about the other.

He wouldn't touch her again until they did. He'd promised himself that. It was too difficult to sample and not take fully. And on those nights he allowed himself to take her with his mind, he left her glowing and satisfied. And left himself oddly unfulfilled.

Still, it was preparing her for him, for the night when he would make those half dreams full reality.

For the night when it was his hands and not his mind on her.

The thought of it had his stomach knotting, his muscles bunching tight. Infuriated with the reaction, he ordered his mind to clear, his body to relax. And was only more infuriated when even his powers didn't calm all the tension.

"The day hasn't come when I can't handle a physical reaction to some pretty half witch," he muttered, and walked back inside his cabin.

Damned if he was going to stand on the porch like some starry-eyed lover and watch for her.

So instead he paced and uttered vile Gaelic curses until he heard the knock on his door.

Mood inexplicably foul, Liam flung open the door. And there she stood, with the sun streaming behind her, a delighted smile on her face, her hair coming loose from her braid and a clutch of tiny purple flowers in her hand.

"Good morning. I think they're wood violets, but I'm not completely sure. I need to buy a book."

She offered them, and Liam felt the heart he was so determined to defend, tremble in his breast. Innocence shined in her eyes, lovely color glowed in her cheeks. And there were wildflowers in her hand.

All he could do was stare. And want.

When he didn't respond, she lowered her hand. "Don't you like flowers?"

"I do, yes. Sorry, I was distracted." For the goddess's sake, get a hold of yourself, Donovan. But even with the order, his scowl was in direct contrast to his words. "Come in, Rowan Murray. You're welcome here, as are your flowers."

"If I've come at a bad time," she began, but he was already stepping back, widening the opening of the door in invitation. "I thought I would come by before I drove into town."

"For more books?" He left the door open, as if to give her a route of escape.

"For those, and to talk to someone about property. I'm thinking of buying some in the area."

"Are you now?" His brow winged up. "Is this the place for you?"

"It seems to be. It could be." She moved her shoulders. "Someplace must be."

"And have you decided—how did you put it— what you'll do to make your living?"

"Not exactly." The light in her eyes dimmed a little with worry. "But I will."

He was sorry to have put that doubt on her face. "I have an idea about that. Come back to the kitchen, and we'll find something to put your little flowers in."

"Have you been in the woods? Everything's starting to pop and bloom. It's wonderful. And all these marvelous flowers around Belinda's cottage. I don't recognize half of them, or the ones around yours."

"Most are simple, and useful for one thing or another." He rooted out a tiny blue vase for the violets as she craned up to peer out his kitchen window.

"Oh, you've more back here. Are they herbs?"

"Aye, herbs they are."

"For cooking."

"For that." A smile tugged at his lips as he slipped the delicate stems into the glass. "And all manner of things. Will you hunt up a book on herbs now?"

"Probably." She laughed and dropped back to the flats of her feet. "There's so much I've never paid attention to. Now I can't seem to find out enough."

"And that includes yourself."

She blinked. "I suppose it does."

"So…" He couldn't resist and pleased himself by toying with the ends of her braid. "What have you found out about Rowan?"

"That she's not as inept as she thought."

His gaze swept back up to hers, sharpened. "And why would you have thought that?"

"Oh, I don't mean about everything. I know how to learn, and how to apply what I learn. I'm organized and practical and I have a good mind. It was the little things and the really big ones I never seemed to know what to do about. Anything in between I handled just fine. But the little things I let go, and the big ones…I always felt I should do what others thought I should do about them."

"I'm about to give you a suggestion on what you'd call a big thing. I expect you to do as you like about it."

"What is it?"

"In a bit," he said with a vague wave of his hand. "Come in here and have a look at what I'm doing."

Baffled, she walked into the adjoining office with him. His computer was up and running, the screen saver swimming with moons and stars and symbols she didn't recognize. He tapped a key and had text popping up.

"What do you think?" he asked her, and she bent forward to read. A moment later she was laughing. "I think I can't read what appears to be computer signals and some foreign language."

He glanced down, let out an impatient huff of breath. He'd gotten so involved in the story line he hadn't considered. Well, that could be fixed. He nearly flicked his wrist to have the straight story line brought up, caught himself not a moment too soon, then made a show of tapping keys while the basic spell ran through his mind.

"There." The screen jiggled, then blipped and brought up new text. "Sit down and read it."

Since nothing would have delighted her more, she did as he asked. It only took a few lines for her to understand. "It's a sequel to Myor." Thrilled, she turned her face up to his. "That's wonderful. You've written another. Have you finished it?"

"If you'd read it you'd see for yourself."

"Yes, yes." This time it was she who waved him away as she settled down to be entertained. "Oh! Kidnapped. She's been kidnapped and the evil warlock's put a spell on her to strip her of her powers."

"Witch," he muttered, wincing a little. "A male witch is still a witch."

"Really? Well… He's locked all her gifts up in a magic box. It's because he's in love with her, isn't it?"

"What?"

"It has to be," Rowan insisted. "Brinda's so beautiful and strong and full of light. He'd want her, and this is his way of forcing her to belong to him.''

Considering, Liam slipped his hands into his pockets. "Is it now?"

"It must be. Yes, here's the handsome warlock— I mean witch who'll do battle with the evil one to get the box of power. It's wonderful."

She all but put her nose to the screen, annoyed she hadn't thought to put on her reading glasses. "Just look at all the traps and spells he'll have to fight just to get to her. Then when he frees her, she won't have any magic to help. Just her wits," Rowan murmured, delighted with the story. "They'll face all this together, risk destruction. Wow, The Valley of Storms. Sounds ominous, passionate. This is what was missing from the first one."

More stunned than insulted, he gaped at her. "Excuse me?"

"It had such wonderful magic and adventure, but no romance. I'm so glad you've added it this time. Rilan will fall madly in love with Brinda, and she with him as they work together, face all these dangers."

Her eyes gleamed as she leaned back and refocused them on Liam. "Then when they defeat the evil witch, find the box, it should be their love that breaks the spell, opens it and gives Brinda back her powers. So they'll live happily ever after."

She smiled a bit hesitantly at the shuttered look in his eyes. "Won't they?"

"Aye, they will." With a few adjustments to the story line, he decided. But that was his task, and for later. By Finn, the woman had it right. "What do you think of the magic dragons in the Land of Mirrors."

"Magic dragons?"

"Here." He bent down, leaning close and manually scrolling to the segment. "Read this," he said and his breath feathered warm across her cheek. "And tell me your thoughts."

She had to adjust her thoughts to block out the quick jump of her pulse, but dutifully focused on the words and read. "Fabulous. Just fabulous. I can just see them flying away on the back of a dragon, over the red waters of the sea, and the mist-covered hills."

"Can you? Show me how you see it—just that. Draw it for me." He pulled her sketchbook out of her bag. "I haven't got a clear image of it."

"No? I don't know how you could write this without it." She picked up a pencil and began to draw. "The dragon should be magnificent. Fierce and beautiful, with wonderful gold wings and eyes like rubies. Long and sleek and powerful," she murmured as she sketched. "Wild and dangerous."

It was precisely what he'd wanted, Liam noted as the drawing came to life under her hand. No tame pet, no captured oddity. She had it exactly: the proud, fierce head, the long powerful body with its wide sweep of wings, the slashing tail, the feel of great movement.

"Do another now." Impatient, he tore off the first sketch, set it aside. "Of the sea and hills."

"All right." She supposed a rough drawing might help him get a more solid visual for his story. Closing her eyes a moment, she brought the image into her mind, that wide, shimmering sea with cresting waves, the jagged rocks that speared silver out of thick swirling mists, the glint of sunlight gilding the edges, and the dark shadow of mountains beyond.

When she was done with it, he ripped that page away as well, demanded she do another. This time of Yilard, the evil witch.

She had great fun with that, grinning to herself as she worked. He should be handsome, she decided. Cruelly so. No wart-faced gnome with a hunched back, but a tall, dashing man with flowing hair and hard dark eyes. She dressed him in robes, imagined they would be red, like a prince.

"Why didn't you make him ugly?" Liam asked her.

"Because he wouldn't be. And if he were, it might seem as if Brinda refused him just because of his looks. She didn't—it was his heart she rejected. The darkness of it that you'd see in the eyes."

"But the hero, he'd be more handsome."

"Of course. We'd expect, even demand that. But he won't be one of those girlishly pretty men with curly gold hair." Lost in the story, she tore off the page herself to begin another. "He'll be dark, dangerous, too. Brave certainly, but not without flaws. I like my heroes human. Still, he risked his life for Brinda, first for honor. And then for love."

She laughed a little as she leaned back from the sketch. "He looks a bit like you," she commented. "But why not? It's your story. Everyone wants to be the hero of their own story after all." She smiled at him. "And it's a wonderful story, Liam. Can I read the rest?"

"Not yet." There were changes to be made now, he thought, and switched off the screen.

"Oh." Disappointment rang in her voice, and fed his ego. "I just want to see what happens after they fly out of the Land Of Mirrors."

"If you do, you'll have to accept my proposition."

"Proposition?"

"A business one. Do the drawings for me. All of them. It's a great deal of work as most of the levels will be complex. I'll need an exacting amount of detail for the graphics, and I'm not easily satisfied."

She held up a hand. She wanted to stop him, to give herself time to find her voice. "You want me to draw the story?"

"It's not a simple matter. I'll require hundreds of sketches, all manner of scenes and angles."

"I don't have any experience."

"No?" He lifted her sketch of the dragon.

"I just tossed those off," she insisted, pushing to her feet with a sense of panic. "I didn't think."

"Is that the way of it?" Interesting. "Fine then, don't think, just draw."

She couldn't keep up, couldn't quite catch her breath. "You can't be serious."

"I'm very serious," he corrected, and laid the sketch down again. "Were you when you said you wanted to do what made you happy?"

"Yes." She was rubbing a hand over her heart, unaware of the movement.

"Then work with me on this if it pleases you.

You'll make the living you need. The Donovan Legacy will see to that part well enough. It's up to you, Rowan.''

''Wait, just wait.'' She kept her hand up, turned away to walk to the window. The sky was still blue, she noted, the forest still green. And the wind blew with the same steady breath.

It was only her life that was changing. If she let it.

To do something she loved for a living? To use it freely and with pleasure and have it give back everything she needed? Could that be possible? Could it be real?

And it was then she realized it wasn't panic hot in her throat, pounding in her blood. It was excitement.

''Do you mean this? Do you think my sketches would suit your story?''

''I wouldn't have said so otherwise. The choice is yours.''

''Mine,'' she said, quietly, like a breath. ''Then, yes, it would please me very much.'' Her voice was slow, thoughtful. But when the full scope of his offer struck, she whirled around, her eyes brilliant. He saw those tiny silver lights in her eyes. ''I'd love to work with you on it. When do we start?''

He took the hand she held out, clasped it firmly in his. ''We just did.''

Later, when Rowan was back in her kitchen celebrating with a glass of wine and a grilled cheese sandwich, she tried to remember if she'd ever been happier.

She didn't think so.

She'd never gotten into town for her books and her house hunting, but that would come. Instead, she mused, she'd found an opening to a new career. One that thrilled her.

She had a chance now, a true and tangible chance for a new direction.

Not that Liam Donovan was going to make it easy. On the contrary, she decided, licking cheese from her thumb. He was demanding, occasionally overbearing and very, very much the perfectionist.

She'd done a full dozen sketches of the gnomes of Firth before he'd approved a single one.

And his approval, as she recalled, had been a grunt and a nod.

Well, that was fine. She didn't need to be patted on the head, didn't require effusive praise. She appreciated the fact that he expected her to be good, that he already assumed they'd make a successful team.

A team. She all but hugged the word to her. That made her part of something. After all these years of quiet wishing, she was telling stories. Not with words; she never had the right words. But with her drawings. The thing she loved most and had convinced herself over the years was an acceptable hobby and no more.

Now it was hers.

Still, she was in many ways a practical woman. She'd cut through her delight to the basics and had discussed terms with him. A pity she wasn't clever enough to have masked her sheer astonishment at the amount he'd told her she'd be paid for the work.

She'd have her house now, she thought, and giggling with glee poured herself a second glass of wine. She'd buy more art supplies, more books. Plants. She'd scout out wonderful antiques to furnish her new home.

And live happily ever after, she thought, toasting herself.

Alone.

She shook off the little pang. She was getting used to alone. Enjoying alone. Maybe she still felt quick pulls and tugs of attraction for Liam, but she understood there would be no acting on them now that they were working together.

He'd certainly demonstrated no sign of wanting a more personal relationship now. If that stung the pride a bit, well, she was used to that, too.

She'd had a terrifying crush on the captain of the debate team her senior year in high school. She could clearly remember those heartbreaking flutters and thrills every time she caught sight of him. And how she'd wished, miserably, she could have been more outgoing, more brightly pretty, more confident, like the girl he'd gone steady with.

Then in college it had been an English major, a poet with soulful eyes and a dark view of life. She'd been sure she could inspire him, lift his soul. When after nearly a full semester he'd finally turned those tragic eyes her way, she'd fallen like a ripe plum from a branch.

She didn't regret it, even though after two short weeks, he'd turned those same tragic eyes to another woman. After all, she'd had two weeks of storybook romance, and had given up her virginity to a man with some sensitivity if no sense of monogamy.

It hadn't taken her long to realize that she hadn't loved him. She'd loved the idea of him. After that his careless rejection hadn't stung quite so deeply.

Men simply didn't find her...compelling, she decided. Mysterious or sexy. And unfortunately, the ones she was most attracted to always seemed to be all of that.

With Liam, he was all of that and more.

Of course, there had been Alan, she remembered. Sweet, steady, sensible Alan. Though she loved him, she'd known as soon as they'd become lovers that she'd never feel that wild thrill with him, that grinding need or that rush of longing.

She'd tried. Her parents had settled on him and it seemed logical that she would gradually fall in love, all the way in love, and make a comfortable life with him.

Hadn't it been the thought of that, a comfortable life, that had finally frightened her enough to make her run?

She could say now she'd been right to do so. It would have been wrong to settle for less than...anything, she supposed. For less than what she was finding now. Her place, her wants, her flaws and her talents.

They wouldn't understand—not yet. But in time they would. She was sure of it. After she was established in a home of her own, with a career of her own, they would see. Maybe, just maybe, they'd even be proud of her.

She glanced at the phone, considered, then shook her head. No, not yet. She wouldn't call her parents and tell them what she was doing. Not quite yet. She didn't want to hear the doubt, the concern, the carefully masked impatience in their voices, and spoil the moment.

It was such a lovely moment.

So when she heard the knock on the front door, she sprang up. It was Liam, had to be Liam. And oh, that was perfect. He'd brought more work, and they could sit in the kitchen and discuss it, toy with it.

She'd make tea, she thought as she hurried through the cabin. A glass and a half of wine was enough if she wanted her mind perfectly clear. She'd had another idea about the Land of Mirrors and how that red sea should reflect when she'd walked home.

Eager to tell him, she opened the door. Her delighted smile of welcome shifted to blank shock.

"Rowan, you shouldn't open the door without seeing who it is first. You're much too trusting for your own good."

With the spring breeze blowing behind him, Alan stepped inside.

Chapter 7

"Alan, what are you doing here?"

She knew immediately her tone had been short and unwelcoming—and very close to accusatory. She could see it in the surprised hurt on his face.

"It's been over three weeks, Rowan. We thought you might appreciate a little face-to-face. And frankly…" He shoved at the heavy sand-colored hair that fell over his forehead. "The tenor of your last phone call worried your parents."

"The tenor?" She bristled, and struggled to fix on a pleasant smile. "I don't see why. I told them I was fine and well settled in."

"Maybe that's what concerns them."

The worry in his earnest brown eyes brought her the first trickle of guilt. Then he took off his coat, laid it neatly over the banister and made a pocket of re-sentiment open under the guilt. "Why would that be a concern?"

"None of us really knows what you're doing up here—or what you hope to accomplish by cutting yourself off from everyone."

"I've explained all of that." Now there was weariness along with the guilt. It was her cottage, damn it, her life. They were being invaded and questioned. But manners had her gesturing to a chair. "Sit down, please. Do you want anything? Tea, coffee?"

"No, I'm fine, but thanks." He did sit, looking stiffly out of place in his trim gray suit and starched white Oxford shirt. He still wore his conservatively striped, neatly Windsor-knotted tie. It hadn't occurred to him to so much as loosen it for the trip.

He scanned the room now as he settled in a chair by the quiet fire. From his viewpoint the cabin was rustic and entirely too isolated. Where was the culture—the museums, the libraries, the theaters? How could Rowan stand burying herself in the middle of the woods for weeks on end?

All she needed, he was certain, was a subtle nudge and she'd pack up and come back with him. Her parents had assured him of it.

He smiled at her, that crooked, slightly confused smile that always touched her heart. "What in the world do you do here all day?"

"I've told you in my letters, Alan." She sat across from him, leaned forward. This time, she was certain, she could make him understand. "I'm taking some time to think, to try to figure things out. I go for long walks, read, listen to music. I've been doing a lot of sketching. In fact—''

"Rowan, that's all well and good for a few days," he interrupted, the patience so thick in his voice her teeth went instantly on edge. "But this is hardly the place for you. It's easy enough to read between the lines of your letters that you've developed some sort of romantic attachment for solitude, for living in some little cottage in the middle of nowhere. But this is hardly Walden Pond."

He shot her that smile again, but this time it failed to soften her. "And I'm not Thoreau. Granted. But I'm happy here, Alan."

She didn't look happy, he noted. She looked irritable and edgy. Certain he could help her, he patted her hand. "For now, perhaps. For the moment. But what happens after a few more weeks, when you realize it's all just a…" He gestured vaguely. "Just an interlude," he decided. "By then it'll be too late to get your position back at your school, to register for the summer courses you planned to take toward your doctorate. The lease is up for your apartment in two months."

Her hands were locked together in her lap now, to keep them from forming fists and beating in frustration on the arms of the chair. "It's not just an interlude. It's my life."

"Exactly." He beamed at her, as she had often seen him beam at a particularly slow student who suddenly grasped a thorny concept. "And your life is in San Francisco. Sweetheart, you and I both know you need more intellectual stimulation than you can find here. You need your studies, your students. What about your monthly book group? You have to be missing it. And the classes you planned to take? And you haven't mentioned a word about the paper you were writing.''

''I haven't mentioned it because I'm not writing it. I'm not going to write it.'' Because it infuriated her that her fingers were beginning to tremble, she wrenched them apart and sprang up. ''And I didn't plan on taking classes, other people planned that for me. The way they've planned every step I've ever taken. I don't want to study, I don't want to teach. I don't want any intellectual stimulation that I don't choose for myself. This is exactly what I've told you before, what I've told my parents before. But you simply refuse to hear.''

He blinked, more than a little shocked at her sudden vehemence. ''Because we care about you, Rowan. Very much.'' He rose as well. His voice was soothing now. She rarely lost her temper, but he understood when she did she threw up a wall no amount of logic could crack. You just had to wait her out.

''I know you care.'' Frustrated, she pressed her fingers to her eyes. ''That's why I want you to hear, I want you to understand, or if understanding is too much, to accept. I'm doing what I need to do. And, Alan—'' She dropped her hands, looked directly into his eyes. ''I'm not coming back.''

His face stiffened, and his eyes went cool as they did when he had outlined a logical premise and she disagreed with him. ''I certainly hoped you'd had enough of this foolishness by now and would fly back

Play the
"LAS VEGAS" Game
and get
3 FREE GIFTS!

FREE GIFTS!

FREE GIFTS!

1. Pull back all 3 tabs on the card at right. Then check the claim chart to see what we have for you — 2 FREE BOOKS and a gift — ALL YOURS! ALL FREE!

2. Send back this card and you'll receive brand-new Silhouette Intimate Moments® novels. These books have a cover price of $4.25 each in the U.S. and $4.75 each in Canada, but they are yours to keep absolutely fre...

3. There's no catch. You're under no obligation to buy anything. We charg nothing — ZERO — for your first shipment. And you don't have to mak any minimum number of purchases — not even one!

4. The fact is thousands of readers enjoy receiving books by mail from the Silhouette Reader Service™. They like the convenience of home delivery... they like getting the best new novels BEFORE they're available in stores... and they love our discount prices!

5. We hope that after receiving your free books you'll want to remain a subscriber. But the choice is yours — to continue or cancel, any time at all! So why not take us up on our invitation, with no risk of any kind. You'll be glad you did!

Yours Free!

© 1998 HARLEQUIN ENTERPRISES LTD.
® and ™ are trademarks owned by Harlequin Books S.A. used under license.

FREE!
No Obligation to Buy!
No Purchase Necessary!

Play the
"LAS VEGAS"
Game

> PEEL BACK HERE ▶
> PEEL BACK HERE ▶
> PEEL BACK HERE ▶

YES! I have pulled back the 3 tabs. Please send me all the free Silhouette Intimate Moments® books and the gift for which I qualify. I understand that I am under no obligation to purchase any books, as explained on the back and opposite page.

345 SDL CT4L   **245 SDL CT4E**

Name	(Please Print Clearly)	

Address		Apt.

City	State/Prov.	Zip/Postal Code

7 7 7 — **GET 2 FREE BOOKS & A FREE MYSTERY GIFT!**

🍀 🍀 🍀 — **GET 2 FREE BOOKS!**

🍒 🍒 🍒 — **GET 1 FREE BOOK!**

🔔 🔔 🔔 — **TRY AGAIN!**

Offer limited to one per household and not valid to current Silhouette Intimate Moments® subscribers. All orders subject to approval.

(S-IM-11/99)

PRINTED IN U.S.A.

The Silhouette Reader Service™ —Here's how it works:

Accepting your 2 free books and gift places you under no obligation to buy anything. You may keep the books and gift and return the shipping statement marked "cancel." If you do not cancel, about a month later we'll send you 6 additional novels and bill you just $3.57 each in the U.S., or $3.96 each in Canada, plus 25¢ delivery per book and applicable taxes if any.* That's the complete price and — compared to the cover price of $4.25 in the U.S. and $4.75 in Canada — it's quite a bargain! You may cancel at any time, but if you choose to continue, every month we'll send you 6 more books, which you may either purchase at the discount price or return to us and cancel your subscription.

*Terms and prices subject to change without notice. Sales tax applicable in N.Y. Canadian residents will be charged applicable provincial taxes and GST.

If offer card is missing write to: Silhouette Reader Service, 3010 Walden Ave., P.O. Box 1867, Buffalo, NY 14240-1867

BUSINESS REPLY MAIL
FIRST-CLASS MAIL   PERMIT NO. 717   BUFFALO, NY

POSTAGE WILL BE PAID BY ADDRESSEE

SILHOUETTE READER SERVICE
3010 WALDEN AVE
PO BOX 1867
BUFFALO NY 14240-9952

NO POSTAGE
NECESSARY
IF MAILED
IN THE
UNITED STATES

with me tonight. I'm willing to find a hotel in the area for a few days, and wait.''

"No, Alan, you misunderstand. I'm not coming back to San Francisco. At all. Not now, not later.''

There, she thought, she'd said it. And a huge weight seemed to lift off her heart. It remained light even when she read the irritation in his eyes.

"That's just nonsense, Rowan. It's your home, of course you'll come back.''

"It's your home, and it's my parents' home. That doesn't make it mine.'' She reached out to take his hands, so happy with her own plans she wanted him to be. "Please try to understand. I love it here. I feel so at home, so settled. I've never really felt like this before. I've even got a job sketching. It's art for a computer game. It's so much *fun*, Alan. So exciting. And I'm going to look into buying a house somewhere in the area. A place of my own, near the sea. I'm going to plant a garden and learn how to really cook and—''

"Have you lost your mind?'' He turned his hands over to grip hers almost painfully. None of the sheer joy on her face registered. Only the words that were to him the next thing to madness. "Computer games? Gardens? Are you listening to yourself?''

"Yes, for the first time in my life that's just what I'm doing. You're hurting me, Alan.''

"I'm hurting you?'' He came as close to shouting as she'd ever heard, and transferred his grip from her hands to her shoulders. "What about what I feel, what I want? Damn it, Rowan, I've been patient with you. You're the one who suddenly and for no reason that made sense decided to change our relationship. One night we're lovers, the next day we're not. I didn't press, I didn't push. I tried to understand that you needed more time in that area.''

She'd bungled things, she realized. She'd bungled it and hurt him unnecessarily out of her inability to find the right words. Even now, she fumbled with them. "Alan, I'm sorry. I'm so sorry. It wasn't a matter of time. It was—"

"I've circled around this incomprehensible snit of yours," he continued, fired up enough to give her a quick shake. "I've given you more room than anyone could expect, believing you wanted a bit more freedom before we settled down and married. Now it's computer games? *Games?* And cabins in the woods?"

"Yes, it is. Alan—"

She was near tears, very near them, had lifted a hand to his chest, not to push him away, but to try to soothe. With a great feral howl, the wolf leaped through the open window. Fangs gleamed white in the lamplight as he sprang, a vicious snarl erupting from his throat.

His powerful forelegs caught Alan just below the shoulders, knocked him back. A table snapped as the combined weight crashed into it. And before Rowan could draw breath, Alan was lying white-faced on the floor with the black wolf snapping at his throat.

"No, no!" Terror gave her both speed and strength. She jumped to them, dived down to wrap her arms around the wolf's neck. "Don't, don't hurt him. He wasn't hurting me."

She could feel the muscles vibrating beneath her, hear the growls rumble like threatening thunder. The horrible image of ripped flesh, pumping blood, screams raced through her head. Without a thought she shifted, pushed her face between them and looked into the wolf's glowing eyes.

There she saw savagery.

"He wasn't hurting me," she said calmly. "He's a friend. He's upset, but he'd never hurt me. Let him up now, please."

The wolf snarled again, and something flashed in his eyes that was almost...human, she thought. She could smell the wildness around him, in him. Very gently she laid her cheek against his. "It's all right now." Her lips grazed his fur. "Everything's all right."

Slowly he moved back. But his body shoved against hers until he stood between her and Alan. As a precaution, she kept a hand on the ruff of his neck as she got to her feet.

"I'm sorry, Alan. Are you hurt?"

"Name of God, name of God." It was all he could manage in a voice that shook. Sheer terror had his muscles weak as water. Each breath burned his lungs, and his chest was bruised where the beast had attacked him. "Get away from it, Rowan. Get back." Though he trembled all over from shock, he crawled to his feet, grabbed a lamp. "Get away, get upstairs."

"Don't you dare hit him." Indignant, she snatched the lamp out of Alan's unsteady hands. "He was only protecting me. He thought you were hurting me."

"Protecting you? For the love of God, Rowan, that's a wolf."

She jerked back when he tried to grab her, then followed instinct and told perhaps the first outright lie of her life. "Of course it's not. Don't be absurd. It's a dog." She thought she felt the wolf jolt under her hand at the claim. Out of the corner of her eye she saw him angle his head up and...well, glare at her. "My dog," she insisted. "And he did precisely what you would expect from a well-trained dog. He protected me against what he saw as a threat."

"A dog?" Staggered and far from convinced he wasn't about to have his throat torn out, Alan shifted his gaze to her. "You have a dog?"

"Yes." The lie was starting to twist around her tongue. "Um. And as you can see, I couldn't be safer here. With him."

"What kind of dog is that?"

"I don't precisely know." Oh, she was a miserably poor liar, she thought. "He's been wonderful company, though, and as you can see I don't have to worry about being alone. If I hadn't called him off, he'd have bitten you."

"It looks like a damn wolf."

"Really, Alan." She did her best to laugh, but it came out thin and squeaky. "Have you ever heard of a wolf leaping through a window, or taking commands from a woman? He's marvelous." She leaned down to nuzzle her face against his fur. "And as gentle with me as a Labrador."

As if in disgust, the wolf shot her one steely look, then walked over to sit by the fire.

"See?" She didn't let her breath shudder out in relief, but she wanted to.

"You never said anything about wanting a dog. I believe I'm allergic." He dug out a handkerchief to catch the first sneeze.

"I never said a lot of things." She crossed to him again, laying her hands on his arms. "I'm sorry for that, I'm sorry I didn't know what to say or how to say it until now."

Alan's eyes kept sliding back toward the wolf. "Could you put him outside?"

Put him outside? she thought, and felt another shaky laugh tickling her throat. The wolf came and went as he pleased. "He's all right, I promise. Come sit down—you're still shaken up."

"Small wonder," he muttered. He would have asked her for a brandy, but imagined she'd have to leave the room to get it. He wasn't risking being alone with that great black hulk.

As if to show the wisdom of this decision, the wolf bared his teeth.

"Alan." Rowan sat on the couch beside him, took his hands in hers. "I am sorry. For not understanding myself soon enough or clearly enough to make you understand. For not being what you'd hoped I would be. But I can't change any of that, and I can't go back to what was."

Alan pushed his heavy hair back again. "Rowan, be reasonable."

"I'm being as reasonable as I know how. I do care for you, Alan, so much. You've been a wonderful friend to me. Now be a friend and be honest. You're not in love with me. It just seemed you should be.''

"Of course I love you, Rowan.''

Her smile was just a little wistful as she brushed back his hair herself. ''If you were *in* love with me, you couldn't have been so reasonable about not sleeping with me anymore.'' Her smile warmed with affection when he fidgeted. ''Alan, we've been good friends, but we were mediocre lovers. There was no passion between us, no urgency or desperation.''

Discussing such a matter quite so frankly embarrassed him. He'd have risen to pace, but the wolf had growled quietly again. ''Why should there be?''

"I don't know, I just know there should. There has to be.'' Thoughtfully she reached up to straighten his tie. ''You're the son my parents always wanted. You're kind, and you're smart and so wonderfully steady. They love both of us.'' She lifted her gaze to his, thought—hoped—she saw the beginnings of understanding there. ''So they assumed we'd cooperate and marry each other. And they convinced you that you wanted the same thing. But do you, Alan, do you really?''

He looked down at their joined hands. ''I can't imagine you not being part of my life.''

"I'll always be part of it.'' She tilted her head, leaned forward and laid her lips on his. At the gesture, the wolf rose, stalked over and snarled. She put an absent hand on his head as she drew back, and studied Alan. ''Did that make your blood swim or your heart flip? Of course not,'' she murmured before he could answer. ''You don't want me, Alan, not the way a man wildly in love wants. You can't make love and passion logical.''

"If you came back, we could try." When she only shook her head, he tightened his grip on her hand. "I don't want to lose you, Rowan. You matter to me."

"Then let me be happy. Let me know that at least one person I matter to, and who matters to me, can accept what I want to do."

"I can't stop you." Resigned now, he lifted his shoulders. "You've changed, Rowan. In three short weeks, you've changed. Maybe you are happy, or maybe you're just playing at being happy. Either way, we'll all be there if you change your mind."

"I know."

"I should go. It's a long drive to the airport."

"I—I can fix you a meal. You can stay the night if you like and go back in the morning."

"It's best if I go now." Skimming a cautious glance toward the hovering wolf, he rose. "I don't know what I think, Rowan, and don't honestly know what I'll say to your parents. They were sure you'd be coming back with me."

"Tell them I love them. And I'm happy."

"I'll tell them—and try to convince them. But since I'm not sure I believe it myself..." He sneezed again, backed away. "Don't get up," he told her, certain it was safer if she kept that light hand on her dog's ferocious head. "I'll let myself out. You ought to get a collar for that thing, at least...make sure he's had his shots and—"

The sneezing fit shook his long, lanky frame so that he walked to the door with the handkerchief over his face. It looked as though the dog was grinning at him, which he knew was ridiculous.

"I'll call you," he managed to say, and rushed out into the fresh air.

"I hurt him." Rowan let out a deep sigh and laid her cheek atop the wolf's head as she listened to the sound of the rental car's engine spring to life. "I couldn't find a way not to. Just like I couldn't find the way to love him." She turned her face, comforting herself with the feel of that warm, soft fur. "You're so brave, you're so strong," she crooned. "And you scared poor Alan half to death."

She laughed a little, but the sound was perilously close to a sob. "Me, too, I guess. You looked magnificent coming through the window. So savage, so fierce. So beautiful. Teeth snapping, eyes gleaming, and that marvelous body fluid as rain."

She slid off the couch to kneel beside him, to burrow against him. "I love you," she murmured, felt him quiver as she caressed him. "It's so easy with you."

They stayed like that for a long, long time, with the wolf staring into the dying fire and listening to her quiet breathing.

Liam kept her busy and kept her close over the next three weeks. She loved the work—and that helped him justify spending so much time with her. It was true enough that most of her sketching could—even should have been done on her own. But she didn't argue when he insisted she come to him nearly every day to work.

It was only to…keep an eye on her, he told himself. To observe her, to help him decide what to do next. And when to do it. It wasn't as if he wanted her company, particularly. He preferred working alone, and certainly didn't need the distraction of her, the scent and the softness. Or the chatter, that was by turns charming and revealing. He certainly didn't need the offerings she so often brought over. Tarts and cookies and little cakes.

As often as not they were soggy or burned—and incredibly sweet.

It wasn't as if he couldn't do without her, very, very easily. That's what he told himself every day as he waited restlessly for her to arrive.

If he went to her nightly in wolf-form, it was only because he understood she was lonely, and that she looked forward to the visits. Perhaps he did enjoy lying beside her on the big canopy bed, listening to her read aloud from one of her books. Watching her fall asleep, invariably with her glasses on and the lamplight shining.

And if he often watched her in sleep, it wasn't because she was so lovely, so fragile. It was only because she was a puzzle that needed to be solved. A problem that required logical handling.

His heart, he continued to assure himself, was well-protected.

He knew the next step was approaching. A time when he would put the choice of what they became to each other in her hands.

Before he did, she would have to know who he was. And what he was.

He could have taken her as a lover without revealing himself. He had done so before, with other women. What business had it been of theirs, after all? His powers, his heritage, his life were his own.

But that might not be the case with Rowan.

She had a heritage of her own, one she knew nothing of. There would also come a time he would have to tell her of that, and convince her of what ran through her blood.

What she would do about it would be her own choice.

The choice to educate her had been his.

But he guarded his heart still. Desire was acceptable, but love was too big a risk.

On the night of the solstice, when magic was thick and the night came late, he prepared the circle. Deep in the woods, he stood in the center of the stone dance. Around him, the air sang, the sweet song of the ancients, the lively tune of the young, the shimmering strains of those who watched and waited.

And the aching harpstrings of hope.

The candles were white and slender, as were the flowers that lay between them. He wore a robe the color of moon-glow belted with the jewels of his rank.

The wind caught his unbound hair as he lifted his face to the last light of the yielding sun. Beams of it fired the trees, shot lances of glimmering gold through the branches to lie like honed swords at his feet.

"What I do here, I do freely, but I make no vow to the woman or to my blood. No duty binds me, no promises made. Hear my voice before this longest day dies. I will call her, and she will come, but I will not use what I have beyond the call. What she sees, what she remembers and believes is for her to decide.''

He watched the silver owl swoop, then perch imperiously on the king stone.

''Father,'' he said, formally and with a bow. ''Your wishes are known, but if I'm ruled by them, would I rule others wisely?''

Knowing that statement would irritate, Liam turned away before the smile could touch his lips. Once more he lifted his face. ''I call Earth.'' He opened his hand to reveal the deep rich soil he held. ''And Wind.'' The breeze rose up high and wild, tossing the earth into a spiral. ''And Fire.'' Two columns of iced blue flame speared up, shivered. ''Witness here what fate will conspire. A song in the blood, the power at hand.''

His eyes began to glow, twin flames against the glowing dark. ''To honor both I've come to this strange land. If she's mine, we both will see. As I will so mote it be.''

Then he turned, lighting each of the candles with a flick of his hand until their flames shot up clear gold and straight as arrows. The wind leaped up, howled like a thousand wolves on the hunt, but remained warm and fragrant with sea and pine and wildflowers.

It billowed the sleeves of his robe, streamed through his hair. And he tasted in it the power of the night.

''Moon rise full and Moon rise white, light her path to me tonight. Guide her here to the circle by the sea. As I will so mote it be.''

He lowered the hands he had flung up to the sky,

and peered through the night, through the trees and the dark, to where she slept restlessly in her bed.

"Rowan," he said with something like a sigh, "it's time. No harm will come to you. It's the only promise I'll make. You don't need to wake. You know the way in your dreams. I'm waiting for you."

Something...called her. She could hear it, a murmur in the mind, a question. Stirring in sleep, she searched for the answer. But there was only wonder.

She rose, stretching luxuriously, enjoying the feel of the silky new nightshirt against her thighs. It was so nice to be out of flannel. Smiling to herself, she slipped into a robe of the same deep blue as her eyes, tucked her feet into slippers.

Anticipation shivered along her skin.

In that half dream, she walked down the steps, trailing her fingertips along the banister. The light in her eyes, the smile on her lips, were those of a woman going to meet her lover.

She thought of him, of Liam, the lover of her dreams, as she walked out of the house and into the swirling white fog.

The trees were curtained behind it, the path invisible. The air, moist and warm on her skin, seemed to sigh, then to part. She moved through it without fear, into that soft white sea of mist with the full white moon riding the sky above, and the stars glimmering like points of ice.

Trees closed in, like sentinels. Ferns stirred in the damp breeze and shimmered with wet. She heard the long, deep call of an owl and turned without thought or hesitation toward the sound. Once, she saw him, huge and grand and as silver as the mist, with the glint of gold on his breast and the flash of green eyes.

Like walking through a fairy tale. A part of her mind recognized, acknowledged and embraced the magic of it, while another part slept, not yet ready to see, not yet ready to know. But her heart beat strong and steady and her steps were quick and light.

If there were eyes peeking from between the lacy branches of the ferns, if there was joyful laughter tinkling down from the high spreading branches of the firs, she could only enjoy it.

At each step, each turn of the path, the fog shimmered clear to open the way for her.

And the water sang quietly.

She saw the lights glowing, little fires in the night. She smelled sea, candle wax, sweet fragrant flowers. Her soft smile spread as she stepped into the clearing, to the dance of stones.

Fog shivered at the edges, like a foamy hem, but didn't slide between stone and candle and flowers. So he stood in the center, on clear ground, his robe white as the moonshine, the jewels belting it flashing with power and light.

If his heart jerked at the sight of her, if it trembled on the edge of where he'd vowed it would not go, he ignored it.

''Will you come in, Rowan?'' he asked and held out a hand.

Something in her yearned. Something in her shuddered. But her smile remained as she took another step. "Of course I will." And walked through the stones.

Something throbbed on the air, along her skin, in her heart. She heard the stones whisper. The lights of the candles flickered, swayed, then flamed straight up again.

Their fingertips brushed. Her eyes stayed on his, trusting, when those fingers linked firm. "I dream of you, every night." She sighed it and would have moved into him but he lay a hand on her shoulder. "And long for you through the days."

"You don't understand, neither the rewards nor the consequences. And you must."

"I know I want you. You've already seduced me, Liam."

A tiny finger of guilt scraped up his spine. "I'm not without needs."

She reached up, cupped his cheek. And her voice was soft where his had been rough. "Do you need me?"

"I want you." Need was too much, too weak, too risky.

"I'm here." She lifted her face to his. "Won't you kiss me?"

"Aye." He leaned down, kept his eyes open and on hers. "Remember this," he murmured when his lips were a breath from hers. "Remember this, Rowan, if you can." And his mouth brushed over hers, once, then again. Testing. Then a gentle nip to make her shiver.

When she sighed, one long quiet breath, he covered her mouth with his, drawing out the moment, the magic, sliding into the taste and texture of her. The warm, slow tangle of tongues thickened his pulse, called to his blood.

On either side of them, the cool blue fire burned bright.

"Hold me. Liam, touch me. I've waited so long."

The sound he made in his throat was caught between growl and groan as he dragged her to him and let his hands roam.

Take her here, take her now, in the circle where we'll be bound. It would be done. That primal urge to cover her, to bury himself in her, warred viciously with his honor. What did it matter what she knew, what she wanted or believed? What did it matter what he gained or lost? There was now, only now, with her hot and eager in his arms and her mouth like a flame against his.

"Lie with me here." Her lips tore from his to race wildly over his face, down his throat. "Make love with me here." She already knew what it would be. Dreams and fantasies danced in her mind, and she knew. Urgent and elemental, fast and potent. And she wanted, wanted, wanted the mad, mindless thrill.

In one rough move, he pushed the robe from her shoulder and set his teeth on that bare flesh. The taste of her swirled through him, drugged wine to cloud the senses. "Do you know who I am?" he demanded.

"Liam." His name was already pounding in her head.

He jerked her back, stared into her dark eyes. "Do you know what I am?"

"Different." It was all she could be sure of, though more, much more hovered at the edge of her senses.

"You're still afraid to know it." And if she feared that, how much more might she fear her own blood? "When you can say it, you'll be ready to give yourself to me. And take what I give you."

Her eyes glowed, deep and blue. Her trembles weren't from fear or cold, but from desire straining for release. "Why isn't this enough?"

He stroked a hand over her hair, soothing her, struggling to soothe himself. "Magic has responsibilities. Tonight, the shortest night, it dances in the forest, sings in the hills of my home, it rides the seas and soars in the air. Tonight it celebrates. But tomorrow, always tomorrow it must remember its purpose. Feel the joy of it."

He kissed her brow, both of her cheeks. "Tonight, Rowan Murray of the O'Mearas, you'll remember what you will. And tomorrow, the choice is yours."

He stepped back, spreading his arms so that the robe whipped around him.

"The night passes, quick and bright, and dawn will break with the softest light. If blood calls to blood come then to me." He paused so that their eyes locked and held. "As you will, so mote it be."

He reached down, took a spray of moonflowers and gave it to her. "Sleep well, Rowan."

The sleeves of his robe fell back, revealing hard muscle. With one flash of power, he sent her from him.

Chapter 8

The sunlight beamed bright through the windows. With a murmur of complaint, Rowan turned from it, pressed her face into the pillow.

Sleep was what she wanted. Sleep where those wonderful and vivid dreams would come, where she could wrap herself in them. There were tatters of them still waving through her mind.

Fog and flowers. Moonbeams and candle-glow. The silver flash of an owl, the quiet roar of the sea. And Liam in a white robe that shimmered with jewels holding her in the center of a circle of stones.

She could taste that hot male flavor of him on her tongue, feel the ripple of muscle held ruthlessly in check, feel the not quite steady thud of his heart against hers.

She had only to slide back into sleep to experience it all again.

But she turned restlessly, unable to find it, or him again.

It was so real, she thought, rubbing her cheek against the pillow to watch the sunbeams shoot in through the windows. So real and so...wonderful. She'd often had very odd and textured dreams, particularly during her childhood.

Her mother had said it was imagination, and that she had a good one. But she needed to learn the difference between what was real, and what was make-believe.

Much too often, Rowan supposed, she'd preferred the make-believe. Because she'd known that had worried her parents a little, she'd buried it. She decided it was because she'd chosen to take her own road now that the dreams were coming back so often.

And it didn't take an expert to understand why her dreams were so often of Liam—and so romantic and erotic. She supposed the wisest course was to simply enjoy them—and not to forget what was real and what wasn't.

She stretched, lifting her arms high, linking her hands. And smiling to herself, replayed what she could remember.

A dream riff on the game they were working on, she thought. With Liam as hero, she as heroine. Magic and mist, romance and denial. A circle of stones that whispered, a ring of candles where the flames rose straight despite the wind. Columns of fire, blue as lake water. Fog that parted as she walked.

Lovely, she mused, then closed her eyes and tried to go back and remember what he'd said to her. She could remember very well the way he'd kissed her. Gently, then with heat and hunger. But what had he said? Something about choices and knowledge and responsibilities.

If she could put it in order she might be able to give him an idea for a story line for another game. But all that was really clear was the way his hands had moved over her—and the needs that had pumped inside her.

They were working together now, she reminded herself. Thinking of him the way she did was both inappropriate and foolish. The last thing she wanted to do was delude herself into thinking he could fall in love with her—the way she was very much aware she could fall in love with him.

So she'd think of the work instead, of the pleasure it gave her. She'd think of the house she meant to buy. It was time to do something about that. But for now, she'd get up, make her coffee, take her morning walk.

She tossed the sheets aside. And there on the bed beside her was a spray of moonflowers.

Her heart took a hard leap into her throat and snapped it shut. Her breath clogged behind it, hot and thick. Impossible, impossible, her mind insisted. But even when she squeezed her eyes tight, she could smell the delicate fragrance.

She must have picked them and forgotten. But she knew there were no such flowers around her cottage or in the woods. Flowers such as she now remembered seeing in her dream, spread like white wishes between the spears of candles.

But it couldn't be. It had been a dream, just another of the dreams that had visited her sleep since she'd come to this place. She hadn't walked through the forest in the night, through the mists. She hadn't gone to that clearing, to Liam or stepped into the stone dance.

Unless…

Sleepwalking, she thought with a quick lick of panic. Had she been sleepwalking? She scrambled out of bed, her gaze glued to the flowers as she grabbed her robe.

And the hem was damp, as if she'd walked through dew.

She clutched the robe against her, as details of the dream raced much too clearly through her mind.

"It can't be real." But the words echoed hollowly. With a sudden flurry of motion, she began to dress.

She ran all the way, not questioning when temper raced with her fear. He'd caused it, that was all she knew. Maybe there was something in that tea he brewed every day. A hallucinogenic of some kind.

It was the only rational explanation. There had to be a rational explanation.

Her breath was short, her eyes huge when she ran up the steps to pound on his door. She gripped the flowers in one white-knuckled hand.

"What did you do to me?" she demanded the moment he opened the door.

He watched her steadily as he stepped back. "Come in, Rowan."

"I want to know what you did to me. I want to know what this means." She thrust the flowers at him.

"You gave me flowers once," he said, almost brutally calm. "I know you've a fondness for them."

"Did you drug the tea?"

Now that calm snapped off into insult. "I beg your pardon?"

"It's the only explanation." She whirled away from him to pace the room. "Something in the tea to make me imagine things, to do things. I'd never walk into the woods at night in my right mind."

"I don't deal in potions of that kind." He added a dismissive shrug that had her trembling with fury.

"Oh, really." She spun back to face him. Her hair tumbling over her shoulders, her eyes snapping vivid blue. "What kind then?"

"Some that ease small hurts of body and soul. But it's not my…specialty."

"And what is your specialty then?"

He shot her a look of impatience. "If you'd open your mind you'd see you already know the answer to that."

She stared into his eyes. As the image of the wolf flashed into her mind, she shook her head and stepped back. "Who are you?"

"You know who I am. And damn it, I've given you plenty of time to deal with it."

"With what? Deal with *what?*" she repeated and stabbed a finger into his chest. "I don't understand anything about you." This time she shoved him and had his own temper peaking. "I don't understand anything about what you expect me to know. I want answers, Liam. I want them now or I want you to leave me alone. I won't be played with this way, or tricked or made a fool of. So you tell me exactly what this means.'' She ripped the flowers back out of his hand. ''Or I'm finished.''

''Finished, are you? Want answers, do you?'' Anger and insult overpowered reason and he nodded. ''Oh aye, then, here's an answer for you.''

_ He threw out his hands. Light, brought on by temper rather than need flashed cold blue from his fingertips. A thin white mist swirled around his body, leaving only those gold eyes bright and clear.

Then it was the eyes of the wolf, glinting at her as he bared his teeth in what might have been a sneer, his pelt gleaming midnight-black.

The blood drained out of her head, left it light and giddy as the mists faded. She could hear in some dim distance, the harsh, ragged sound of her own breath and the trembling scream that sounded only in her mind.

She stepped back, staggered. Her vision grayed at the edges. Tiny lights danced in front of her eyes.

When her knees buckled, he cursed ripely, and his hands caught her before she could fall.

''Damn if you'll faint and make me feel like a monster.'' He eased her into a chair and shoved her head between her knees. ''Catch your breath, and next time have a care with what you wish for.''

There was a hive of bees buzzing in her head, a hundred icy fingers skimming over her skin. She babbled something when he lifted her head. She would have pulled back, but he had his hands firm on her face. ''Just look,'' he murmured, gently now. ''Just look at me. Be calm.''

Awake and aware this time, she felt his mind touch her. Instinct had her struggling, had her hands lifting to push at him.

"No, don't fight me on this. I won't harm you."

"No...I know you won't." She knew that, was inexplicably certain of it. "Could I—could I have some water?"

She blinked at the glass she hadn't known was in his hand, hesitated and saw that flicker of annoyance in his eyes. "It's only water. You've my word on it."

"Your word." She sipped, let out a shaky breath. "You're a..." It was too ridiculous, but she'd seen. For Lord's sake, she'd seen. "You're a werewolf."

His eyes rounded in what could only be shock, then he shoved himself to his feet to stare at her in baffled fury. "A werewolf? For the love of Finn where do you come up with these things? A werewolf." He muttered it now as he prowled the room. "You're not stupid, you're just stubborn. It's the broad light of day, isn't it? Do you see a full moon out there? Did I come snapping at your throat?"

He muttered curses in Gaelic as he whirled back around to glare at her. "I'm Liam of Donovan," he said with pride ringing in his voice. "And I'm a witch."

"Oh, well then." Her laugh was quick and lightly hysterical. "That's all right then."

"Don't cringe from me." He snapped it out, cut to the core when she hugged her arms over her chest. "I've given you time to see, to prepare. I'd not have shown you so abruptly if you hadn't pushed me."

"Time to see? To prepare? For *this?*" She ran an

unsteady hand through her hair. "Who could? Maybe I'm dreaming again," she murmured, then bolted straight in the chair. "Dreaming. Oh, my God."

He saw her thoughts, jammed his hands into his pockets. "I took nothing you weren't willing to give."

"You made love to me—you came to my bed while I slept and—"

"My mind to your mind," he interrupted. "I kept my hands off you—for the most part."

The blood had come back into her face and flamed there now. "They weren't dreams."

"They were dreams right enough. You'd have given me more than that, Rowan. We both know the truth of it. I won't apologize for dreaming with you."

"Dreaming with me." She ordered herself to her feet, but had to brace a hand on the chair to stay on them. "Am I supposed to believe this?"

"Aye." A smile ghosted around his mouth. "That you are."

"Believe you're a witch. That you can change into a wolf and come into my dreams whenever you like."

"Whenever you like as well." A different tack, he mused, might be in order. One that would please them both. "You sighed for me, Rowan. Trembled for me." He moved forward to skim his hands up her arms. "And smiled in your sleep when I left you."

"What you're talking about happens in books, in the games you write."

"And in the world as well. You've been in that world. I've taken you there. You remember last night, I can see it in you mind."

"Don't look in my mind." She jerked back, mortified because she believed he could. "Thoughts are private things."

"And yours are often so clear on your face I don't have to look any further. I won't look further if it upsets you."

"It does." She caught her bottom lip between her teeth. "You're a psychic?"

He blew out a huff of breath. "I've the power to see, if that's your meaning. To brew a spell, to call the thunder." He shrugged negligently, elegantly. "To shift shapes at my will."

Shape-shifter. Good God. She'd read of such things, of course she had. In novels, in books on myths and legends. It couldn't be real. And yet...could she deny what she'd seen with her own eyes? What she knew in her own heart?

"You came to me as the wolf." If she was mad, she thought, she might as well have mad answers.

"You weren't afraid of me then. Others would have been, but not you. You welcomed me in, put your arms around me, wept on my neck."

"I didn't know it was you. If I'd known—" She broke off as other memories crept back. "You watched me undress! You sat there while I was in the tub."

"It's a lovely body you have. Why should you be shamed that I've seen it? Only hours ago you asked me to touch you."

"That's entirely different."

Something that might have been reluctant amusement flickered in his eyes. "Ask me to touch you now, knowing, and it will be even more different."

She swallowed hard. "Why haven't you...touched me already?"

"You needed time to know me, and yourself. I've no right to take innocence, even when it's offered, when no knowledge goes with it."

"I'm not innocent. I've been with men before."

Now there was something dark shimmering in his eyes, something not quite tame. But his voice was even when he spoke. "They didn't touch your innocence, didn't change it. I will. If you lie with me, Rowan, it'll be as the first time. I'll give you pleasure that will make you burn...."

His voice had lowered. When he traced a finger down her throat she shivered, but didn't step back. Whoever—whatever—he was, he moved her. He called to her. "What will you feel?"

"Delight," he murmured, easing closer to brush his mouth over her cheek. "Demand. Desire. It's the passion you wanted that you didn't find in others. Urgency, you said. And desperation. I feel that for you, whether I will or no. That much power you have over me. Is it enough for you?"

"I don't know. No one's ever felt that for me."

"I do." He brought his hands over, slipped the first two buttons free on her simple cotton shirt. "Let me see you, Rowan. Here, in the light of day."

"Liam." It was insanity. How could it be real? Yet everything she felt was too intense, too immediate to be otherwise. Nothing, she realized with a dull sense of shock, had ever been more real to her. ''I believe this.'' Her breath trembled free. ''I want this.''

He looked in her eyes, saw both the fear and the acceptance. ''So do I.''

The skim of his knuckles over her skin left a hot trail down her skin as he unbuttoned her blouse, slipped it off her shoulders. Her heart tumbled in her chest as he smiled. ''You were in a hurry this morning,'' he murmured, noting she hadn't taken the time for a bra.

To please himself he traced a fingertip lightly down the subtle slope, over the tip, and watched her eyes go opaque. ''You know I can't stop you,'' she said, watching him.

''Aye, you can.'' Through sheer will he kept his touch gentle. ''With but a word. I hope you won't for it'll drive me mad not to have you now. Do you want me to touch you?''

''Yes.'' More than she wanted to breathe.

''You said once that it shouldn't be simple.'' With his eyes on hers, he unbuttoned her jeans. ''It won't be.'' Skilled fingertips skimmed under denim to tease, to awaken. ''Not for either of us.''

It was like a dream, she thought. Just one more glorious dream. ''Why do you want this?''

''Because you're in my mind, in my blood.'' That much was true, but he told himself he could block her out of his heart. Leaning forward, he caught her jaw gently between his teeth. ''I'm in yours.''

Why should she deny it? Why shouldn't she accept, even embrace these outrageous sensations, this heat in the belly and flutter in the pulse? He was what she wanted, with a giddy greed she'd felt for no other man.

So take, her mind murmured, and pay whatever price is asked.

Still her fingers shook slightly as she tugged his shirt over his head. Then, with a kind of wonder, she spread her hands over his chest.

Hard, warm. Strength just on the edge of danger held ruthlessly in check. She knew it, even as her curious fingers traced up, over broad shoulders, down the taut muscles of his arms. She heard the soft feline purr before she realized it had come from her own throat.

Her gaze shot up to his, and in her eyes was a mix of shock and delight. "I've done this before...in my dreams."

"With much the same results." He'd intended his tone to be dry, but there was an edge to it that stunned him. Gently, he ordered himself, she should be treated gently. "Will you move beyond dreams now, Rowan, and lie with me?"

For an answer she stepped to him, rising onto her toes so that her mouth met his. The beauty of that, just that, had his arms coming hard around her. "Hold tight," he murmured.

She felt the air shudder, heard a rustle of wind. There was a sensation of rising, spinning, then tumbling all in the space of a single heartbeat. Before fear could fully form, before the gasp of it could shudder from her mouth to his, she was lying beneath him, dipped deep into a bed soft as clouds.

Her eyes flew open. She could see the polished

beams of a wood ceiling, the stream of sunlight. "But how—"

"I've magic for you, Rowan." His mouth moved to the vulnerable flesh of her throat. "All manner of magic."

They were in his bed, she realized. In the blink of an eye they'd moved from one room to another. And now his hands...oh, sweet Lord, how could the simple touch of flesh to flesh cause such *feeling?*

"Give me your thoughts." His voice was rough, his hands light as air. "Let me touch them, and show you."

She opened her mind to him, gasping when she not only felt the heat of his body, the skim of his hands, but saw, the images forming out of the mists in her mind, the two of them tangled together on a huge, yielding bed in a path of early summer sunlight.

Every sensation now, every shimmering layer was reflected back, as if a thousand silver mirrors shone out of her heart. And so with a kiss only, one long, drugging kiss, he brought her softly to peak.

She moaned out the pleasure of it, the sheer wonder of having her body slide over a velvet edge. Her thoughts scattered, dimmed, reformed in a mixed maze of colors, only to fly apart again as his teeth grazed her shoulder.

She was beyond price. An unexpected treasure in her openness, her utter surrender to him and to her own pleasures. Now, at last now his hands could take, his mouth could feast. Soft, silky flesh, pale as the moon, delicate curves and subtle scents.

The animal that beat in his blood wanted to ravage,

to grasp and plunge. She would not deny him. Knowing that, he wrapped the chain tighter around his own pounding throat and offered only tenderness.

She moved beneath him, all quiet sighs and luxurious stretches. Her hands roamed over him freely, building and banking small fires. Dark and heavy, her eyes met his when he lifted his head.

And her lips curved slowly.

"I've waited so long to feel like this." She lifted a hand to slide her fingers through his hair. "I never knew I was waiting."

Love waits.

The words came back to him like a drumbeat, a warning, a whisper. Ignoring it, he lowered again to take her breast with his mouth. She arched, gave a little cry as the movement had been sudden and just a bit rough.

Then she groaned, and the hand that had combed lazily through his hair fisted tight, pressing him urgently against her. Heat flashed, a quick bolt to the center. His tongue tormented, his teeth hinted of pain. She gave herself over to it, to him, trembling again as both mind and body steeped in pleasure.

No one had ever touched her this way, so deep it seemed he knew her needs and secrets better than she herself. Her heart quaked, then soared under his quietly ruthless mouth. And opened wide as love flooded it.

She clung to him now, murmuring mindlessly as they rolled over the bed, as flesh grew damp with desire and minds misted with delight.

She was…glory, he thought dimly while he tumbled to a depth he'd never explored with a woman. His keen senses were barraged with her. Scent like spice on the wind, taste like honeyed wine, texture like heated silk. Whatever he asked for she gave, a rose opening petal by petal.

She rose up when he reached for her, her body impossibly fluid, her lips like a flame on his shoulder, across his chest, against his greedy mouth.

Against his hand she was warm and wet, and her body arched back like a drawn bow when his fingers found her. Eyes sharp on her face, he watched that fresh rush of shock and pleasure and fear flicker over hers as he took her up, urged her over.

Her breath sobbed out, her body shook as that new arrow of sensation pinned her, left her quivering helplessly. Even as her head dropped limply on the shoulder her nails had just bit into, he sent her spinning up again.

When they tumbled back, he gripped her hands, waited for his vision to clear, waited for her eyes to open and meet his. The air dragged in and out of his lungs. ''Now.''

The word was nearly an oath as he drove into her.

Held there, held quivering to watch her eyes go wide and blind. Held there, held gasping while the thrill of filling her burned in his blood.

Then she began to move.

A lift of the hips, a falling away that drew him down. Slow, achingly slow, with a low moan for each long, deep thrust.

It was his eyes, only his eyes she saw now, brilliantly gold, stunningly intense as they took each other to a secret space where the air fluttered like velvet on the skin. Her fingers clung to his, her eyes stayed open and aware. Every pulse that beat in her body gathered into one steady throb that filled the heart to bursting.

When it burst, and her mind and body with it, she arched high and hard against him, called out his name with a kind of wonder. Saying hers, he buried his face in her hair and dived with her.

He stretched over her, his head between her breasts, his long body lax. She kept her eyes closed, the better to hold on to that sensation of flying, of falling. Never before had she been so aware, so in tune with her own desires or with a man's.

And never, she realized, had she been so willing, even eager, to surrender to both.

A small smile curved her lips as she lazily stroked his hair. In her mind she could see them together there. Wantonly sprawled, naked, damp and tangled.

She wondered how long it would be before he'd want to touch her again.

"I already do." Liam's voice was thick and low. His tongue skimmed carelessly over the side of her breast and made her shiver.

"Thoughts are private."

She was so soft and warm in the afterglow of love, and that lazy sip of her flesh so delightful. He slid a hand up, molded her gently and shifted to nibble. "I've been inside your thoughts." Her nipple hardened against a flick of his tongue and needs stirred again. "I've been inside you, *a ghra*. What's the point of secrets now?"

"Thoughts are private," she repeated, but the last word ended on a moan.

"As you wish." He slipped out of her mind even as he slipped into her.

She must have slept. Though she remembered nothing but curling around him after that second, surprising slide into heaven. She stirred in bed, and found herself alone.

Sunny morning had become rainy afternoon. The sound of its steady patter, the golden haze that seemed to linger inside her body, both urged her to simply snuggle back and sleep again.

But curiosity was stronger. This was his bed, she thought, smiling foolishly. His room. Shoving at her tangled hair, she sat up and looked.

The bed was amazing. A lake of feathers covered in smooth, silky sheets, backed by a headboard of dark polished wood carved with stars and symbols and lettering she couldn't make out. Idly she traced her fingers in the grooves.

He, too, had a fireplace facing the bed. It was fashioned of some kind of rich green stone and topped by a mantel of the same material. Gracing that were colorful crystals. She imagined their facets would catch the sun brilliantly. Fat white candles stood at one end in a triad.

There was a tall chair with its back carved in much the same way as the headboard. A deep blue throw woven with crescent moons was tossed over one of its arms.

The tables by the bed held lamps with bases of bronze mermaids. Charmed, she ran a finger along the curving tails.

He kept the furnishings spare, she noted, but he chose what he kept around him with care.

She rose, stretched, shook back her hair. The rain made her feel beautifully lazy. Instead of looking for her clothes, she walked to his closet hoping she would find a robe to bundle into.

She found a robe, and it made her fingers jerk on the door. A long white robe with wide sleeves.

He'd worn it the night before. In the stone dance. Under the moonlight. A witch's robe.

Closing the door quickly, she spun around, looked around wildly for her clothes. Downstairs, she remembered with a jolt. He'd undressed her downstairs, and then...

What was she doing? What was she thinking of? Was this real or had she gone mad?

Had she just spent hours in bed with him?

And if it was real, if what she'd always thought was fantasy was suddenly truth, had he used it to lure her here?

For lack of anything else, she snatched up the throw, wrapped it around herself. She grasped the ends tight as the door of the bedroom opened.

He lifted a brow when he saw her, draped in the cloth his mother had woven for him when he'd turned twenty-one. She looked tumbled and lovely and outrageously desirable. He took a step toward her before he caught the glint of suspicion in her eyes.

Annoyed, he moved past her to set the tea tray he'd carried up on the bedside table. "What have you thought of that I haven't explained?"

"How can you explain what should be impossible?"

"What is, is," he said simply. "I am a hereditary witch, descended from Finn of the Celts. What powers I have are my birthright."

She had to accept that. She had seen, she had felt. She kept her shoulders straight and her voice even. "Did you use those powers on me, Liam?"

"You ask me not to touch your thoughts. Since I respect your wishes, try to be more specific in your questions." Obviously irritated, he sat on the side of the bed and picked up a cup of tea.

"I was attracted to you, strongly and physically attracted to you from the first minute. I behaved with you as I've never behaved with a man. I've just gone to bed with you and felt things..." She took a long, steadying breath as he watched her, as she saw a little gleam that had to be triumph light his eyes. "Did you put a spell on me to get me into bed?"

The gleam went dark, and triumph became fury so swiftly she stumbled back a step in instinctive defense. China cracked on wood as he slammed the cup down. From somewhere not so far away, came the irritable grumble of thunder.

But he got to his feet slowly, like a wolf, she thought, stalking prey.

"Love spells, love potions?" He came toward her.

She backed away. "I'm a witch not a charlatan. I'm a man not a cheat. Do you think I would abuse my gifts, shame my name for sex?"

He made a dismissive gesture; the window shuddered and cracked, giving her a clue just how dangerous was his temper. "I didn't ask for you, woman. Whatever part fate played in it, you came to this place, and to me, of your own will. And you're free to go in the same manner."

"How can you expect me not to wonder?" she shot back. "I'm just supposed to shrug and accept. Oh, Liam's a witch. He can turn into a wolf and read my mind and blink us from one room to the next whenever he likes. Isn't that handy?"

She whirled away from him, the throw flicking out around her bare legs. "I'm an educated woman who's just been dropped headfirst into some kind of fairy tale. I'll ask whatever questions I damn well please."

"You appeal to me when you're angry," he murmured. "Why is that, I wonder?"

"I have no idea." She spun back. "I don't *get* angry, by the way. And I never shout, but I'm shouting at you. I don't fall naked into bed with men or have arguments wearing nothing but a blanket, so if I ask if you've done something to make me behave this way, I think it's a perfectly logical question."

"Perhaps it is. Insulting, but logical. The answer is no." He said it almost wearily as he went back to sit on the bed and sip his tea. "I cast no spell, wove no magic. I'm Wiccan, Rowan. There is one law we live by, one rule that cannot be broken. 'An it harm none.' I will do nothing to harm you. And my pride alone would prevent me from influencing your response to me. What you feel, you feel.''

When she said nothing, he moved his shoulder in a careless jerk, as if there wasn't a sharp clawed fist around his heart. ''You'll want your clothes.'' With no more than those words, her jeans and shirt appeared on the chair.

She let out a short laugh, shook her head. ''And you don't think I should be dazzled by something like that. You expect a great deal, Liam.''

He looked at her again, thought of what ran in her blood. Not nearly ready to know, he decided, annoyed with his own impatience. ''Aye, I suppose I do. You have a great deal, Rowan, if you'd only trust yourself.''

''No one's ever really believed in me.'' Steady now, she walked to him. ''That's a kind of magic you offer me that means more than all the flash and wonder. I'll start with trusting this much—I'll believe that what I feel for you is real. Is that enough for now?''

He lifted a hand to lay it over the one that held the ends of the throw. The tenderness that filled him was new, unexplained and too sweet to question. ''It's enough. Sit, have some tea.''

''I don't want tea.'' It thrilled her to be so bold, to loosen her grip and let the throw fall away. ''And I don't want my clothes. But I do want you.''

Chapter 9

She was under a spell. Not one that required incantations, Rowan thought dreamily. Not one that called on mystical powers and forces. She was in love, and that, she supposed, was the oldest and the most natural of magics.

She'd never been as comfortable nor as uneasy with any other man. Never been quite so shy, nor ever so bold as she was with Liam. Looking back, gauging her actions, her reactions, her words and her wishes, she realized she'd fallen under that spell the moment she'd turned and seen him behind her on the cliffs.

The wind in his hair, annoyance in his eyes, Ireland in his voice. That graceful, muscular body with its power held ruthlessly in check.

Love at first sight, she thought. Just one more page of her own personal fairy tale.

And after love, her love, they'd found their way to

a friendship she treasured every bit as much. Companionship, an ease of being. She knew he enjoyed having her with him, for work, for talk, for sitting quietly and watching the sky change with evening.

She could tell by the way he smiled at her, or laughed, or absently brushed a hand through her hair.

At times like that she could sense that restlessness that prowled in him shifting into a kind of contentment. The way it had, she remembered, when he'd come to her as a wolf and laid down beside her to listen to her read.

Wasn't it odd, she mused, that in searching for her own peace of mind, she'd given him some?

Life, she decided as she settled down to sketch a line of foxglove on the banks of the stream, was a wonderful thing. And now, finally, she was beginning to live it.

It was lovely to do something she enjoyed, to sit in a place that made her happy and spend time exploring her own talents, to study the way the sun filtered through the treetops, the way the narrow ribbon of water curved and sparkled.

All these shades of green to explore, the shapes of things, the marvelously complicated bark of a Douglas fir, the charming fancy of a lush fern.

There was time for them now, time for herself.

No longer was she required to get up in the morning and put on a neat, conservative suit, to wade through morning traffic, drive through the rain with a briefcase full of papers and plans and projects in the seat beside her. And to stand at the front of the classroom knowing that she wasn't quite good enough, certainly not dedicated enough an instructor as each one of her students deserved.

She would never again have to come home every evening to an apartment that had never really felt like home, to eat her solitary dinner, grade her papers, go to bed. Except for every Wednesday and Sunday when she would be expected for dinner by her parents. They would discuss their respective weeks, and she would listen to their advice on the direction of her career.

Week after week, month after month, year after year. It was hardly any wonder they'd been so shocked and hurt when she'd broken that sacred routine. What would they say if she told them she'd gone way beyond the scope of any imaginings and had fallen headlong in love with a witch? A shape-shifter, a magician. A wonder.

The idea made her laugh, shake her head in delighted amusement. No, she thought, it was best to keep certain areas of her new life all to herself.

Her much-loved and decidedly earthbound parents would never believe, much less understand it.

She couldn't understand it herself. It was real, it was true, there was no way to deny it. Yet how could he be what he claimed to be? How could he do what she had seen him do?

Her pencil faltered, and she reached up to toy nervously with the end of her braid. She *had* seen it, less than a week ago. And since then there had been a dozen small, baffling moments.

She'd seen him light candles with a thought, pluck a white rose out of the air, and once—in one of his rare foolish moods—he'd whisked her clothes away with no more than a grin.

It amazed and delighted her. Thrilled her. But she could admit here, alone, in her deepest thoughts, that part of her feared it as well.

He had such powers. Over the elements, and over her.

He'll never use them to harm you.

The voice in her head made her jolt so that her sketchpad slapped facedown on the forest floor. Even as she pressed a hand to her jumping heart she saw the silver owl swoop down. He watched her from the low branch of a tree out of unblinking eyes of sharp green. Gold glinted against the silver of his breast.

Another page from the fairy tale, she thought giddily and managed to get to her feet. "Hello." It came out as a croak, forcing her to clear her throat. "I'm Rowan."

She bit back a shriek as the owl spread his regal wings, soared down from the tree and with a ripple of silver light, became a man.

"I know well enough who you are, girl." There was music and magic in his voice, and the echo of green hills and misty valleys.

Her nerves were forgotten in sheer pleasure. "You're Liam's father."

"So I am." The stern expression on his face softened into a smile. He moved toward her, footsteps silent in soft brown boots. And taking her hand, lifted it gallantly to kiss. "It is a pleasure to be meeting you, young Rowan. Why do you sit here alone, worrying?"

"I like to sit alone sometimes. And worrying's one of my best things."

He shook his head, gave a quick snap of his fingers and had her sketchpad fluttering up into his hand. "No, this is." He sat comfortably on the fallen tree, cocking his head so that his hair flowed like liquid silver to his shoulders. "You've a gift here, and a charming one." He gave the space beside him an absent pat. "Sit yourself," he said when she didn't move. "I'll not eat you."

"It's all so...dumbfounding."

His gaze shifted to hers with honest puzzlement lighting the green. "Why?"

"Why?" She was sitting on a tree in the woods beside a witch, the second she'd met so far. "You'd be used to it, but it's just a little surprising to a mere mortal."

His eyes narrowed, and if Rowan had been able to read his mind she'd have been stunned to read his quick and annoyed thoughts aimed at his son. *The stubborn whelp hasn't told her yet. What is he waiting for?*

Finn had to remind himself it was Liam's place and not his own and smiled at Rowan again.

"You've read stories, haven't you? Heard legends and songs that speak of us?"

"Yes, of course, but—"

"And where, young Rowan, do you think stories and legends and songs come from if not from grains of truth?" He gave her hand a fatherly pat. "Not that truth doesn't all too often become stretched and twisted. There you have witches tormenting innocent young children, popping them into ovens for dinner. Do you think we're after baking you up for a feast?''

The amusement in his voice was contagious. "No, of course not."

"Well then, stop your fretting." Dismissing her concerns he paged through her sketches. "You'll do well here. You do well here." His grin flashed as he came to one with faerie eyes peeking through a thick flood of flowers. "Well and fine here, girl. Why is it you don't use colors?"

"I'm no good with paints," she began. "But I thought I might get some chalks. I haven't done much with pastels and thought it might be fun."

He made a sound of approval and continued to flip pages. When he came to one of Liam standing spread-legged and arrogant on the cliffs, he grinned like a boy. And there was pride in his eyes, in his voice. "Oh, this is like him, isn't it? You've got him."

"Have I?" she murmured, then flushed when that green gaze rested on her face again.

"Every woman has power, Rowan. She's only to learn to use it. Ask him for something."

"For what?"

"What pleases you." Then he tapped a finger on the page. "Will you give me this? For his mother."

"Yes, of course." But when she started to tear the page out, it vanished.

"She misses him," Finn said simply. "Good day to you, Rowan of the O'Mearas."

"Oh, but won't you—" He was gone before she could ask him to walk to Liam's with her. " "There are more things on heaven and earth, Horatio,''' she murmured, and rising, walked to Liam's alone.

He wasn't waiting for her. That's what he told himself. He had a great deal to occupy his mind and fill his time. He certainly wasn't roaming aimlessly around the house waiting for a woman. Wishing for her.

Hadn't he told her he didn't intend to work that day? Hadn't he said that specifically, so they'd each have a little time apart? They both required their little pieces of solitude, didn't they?

So where the devil was she? he wondered as he roamed aimlessly around the house.

He could have looked, but it would be too undeniable an admission that he wanted her there. And she had been very clear about her expectations of privacy. No one knew or respected the need for privacy more.

And he was giving it to her, wasn't he? He didn't follow the urge just to take a quick glance into the glass and see, or skim lightly into her thoughts.

Damn it.

He could call her. He stopped his restless pacing and considered. A quiet murmur of her name on the air. It was hardly an intrusion, and she was free to ignore it if she wished. Tempted, sorely tempted, he moved to the door, opened it to step out into the balmy air.

But she wouldn't ignore it, he thought. She was too generous, too giving. If he asked, she'd come. And if he asked, it would be like an admission of weakness for her.

It was only a physical need yet, he assured himself. Just a longing for the taste of her, the shape, the scent. If it was sharper than was comfortable it was likely due to his own restraint.

He'd been gentle with her, always. No matter how his blood burned, he'd treated her carefully. When every instinct clawed at him to take more, he'd held back.

She was tender, he reminded himself. It was his responsibility to control the tone of their lovemaking, to yank back the fury of it less he frighten her.

But he wanted more, craved it.

Why shouldn't he have it? Liam jammed his hands into his pockets and strode up and down the porch. Why the devil shouldn't he do as he pleased with her? If he decided—and it was still his decision to make— to accept her as a mate, she would have to accept him as well. All aspects of him.

He'd had enough of waiting around while she was off somewhere ignoring him. As he paced, his temper and the passion stirring to life beneath grew more fierce and more restless. And he'd had enough of minding his step with her.

It was time she knew what she was dealing with— in him and in herself.

"Rowan Murray," he muttered, and his eyes seared the air. "You'd best be ready for the likes of me."

He flung up his arms. The flash of light that snapped out, simmered to a glow as he reformed on her porch.

And knew immediately she wasn't there.

He snarled, cursed, furious with himself, not only for the act that had demonstrated his need for her, but with her for not being exactly where he expected her to be.

By the goddess, he could fix that, couldn't he?

Rowan smiled as she stepped out of the trees. She could hardly wait to tell Liam she'd met his father. She imagined they would settle down in the kitchen where he would tell her stories about his family. He had such a marvelous way of telling stories. She could listen to that musical rise and fall of his voice for hours.

And now that she'd met his father, there might be a way to ask him if she could meet other members of his family. He'd mentioned cousins from time to time, so...

She stopped, staggered with the sudden realization. Belinda. For heaven's sake, he'd told her that first day that he and Belinda were related. Didn't that mean Belinda was...

"Oh!" With a laugh Rowan turned in a circle. "Life is just astonishing."

As she said it, as her laughter rose up, the air shook. The pad fell out of her hands for the second time that day as she raised her hands to her throat. Earthquake? she thought with a dim, dizzy panic.

She felt herself spin, the wind gallop. Light, bright and blinding, flashed in front of her eyes. She tried to call out for Liam, but the words stuck in her throat.

Then she was crushed against him, lights still whirling, wind still rushing as his mouth ravaged hers.

She couldn't get her breath, couldn't find a single coherent thought. Her heart boomed in her chest, in her head as she struggled for both. Suddenly her feet were dangling in the air as he yanked her off them with a strength that was both casual and terrifying.

His mouth was brutal on hers, hard and greedy as it swallowed her gasps. He was in her mind as well, tangled in her thoughts, ruthlessly seducing it as he ruthlessly seduced her body. Unable to separate the two, she began to shake.

"Liam, wait—"

"Take what I give you." He dragged her head back by the hair so that she had one terrifying glimpse of the fire in his eyes. "Want what I am."

He savaged her throat, spurred on by each helpless whimper. And with his mind drove her violently to peak. When she cried out, he fell with her onto the bed. Her hair tumbled free as he liked it best, spread out around her head like a gleaming lake. Her eyes were wide, the passion that rode with the fear turning them midnight-dark.

"Give me what I need."

When her mind whispered yes, he took it.

Heat came in floods, sensations struck like fists. All was a confused mass of wrenching feelings as he drove her beyond the civilized. He was the wolf now, she thought, as he tore at her clothes. If not in form, in temperament. Savage and wild. She heard the growl sound in his throat as he bared her breast to his mouth.

Then she heard her own scream. And it was one of glory.

No time to float or to sigh. Only to race and to moan with every nerve inside her scraped raw and sparking. Her breath heaved out of tortured lungs, her body arched and twisted, energized by every new outrageous demand.

His hands bruised her, his teeth nipped and each separate, small pain was the darkest of pleasures.

And somewhere inside her came the answering call for more.

He yanked her up so that they knelt on the bed, torso to torso, and his hands could find more. Take more. Freed, the animal inside him devoured, and it ravaged. And still it hunted.

Hands slipped over flesh slick with sex. Mouths met like thunder. They rolled over the bed, locked and lost together. Desire had fangs, and a voice that howled like a beast.

He drove her up again, hard and fast so that she wept out his name, so that her body shuddered and her nails clawed at him. She gasped for air, felt it sear her throat and struggled to find some steady ground.

Then he found her with his mouth.

She went wild beneath him, bucking, arching. Her head whipped from side to side as she clawed at the bedclothes, his hair, his back. With tongue and teeth he drove both of them mad, shuddering himself when the orgasm ripped through her, when her body rose up with it like a flame, then melted, slow and soft as candle wax.

"You'll come with me." He panted it out as he moved up her body with hot, greedy kisses over still-quivering flesh. With one jerk, he lifted her hips, opened her to him.

Then plunged.

Hot, hard, fast, their bodies and minds climbed together. He buried himself deep, locking his teeth on her shoulder as he drove into her with savage thrusts. Mindlessly she locked around him, hungering for each dark and dangerous thrill. Energy pumped through her, wild and sweet, so her movements and demands were as fierce as his.

Blood called to blood and heart to heart. With one last violent stroke, with one low feral cry he emptied into her. And she willingly let herself come apart.

He was too appalled to speak, too stunned to move. He knew he weighed heavily on her, could feel the quick, hard trembles that shook her beneath him. Her breath sounded short and harsh in his ear and shamed him.

He'd used her without control.

Deliberately, purposefully, selfishly.

It was perfectly clear that he'd allowed himself to rationalize it for his own needs, and giving her no choice had taken her like a beast rutting in the woods.

He'd sacrificed compassion for passion, kindness for a momentarily physical release.

Now he had to face the consequences: her fear of him and his own discarding of his most sacred vow.

He rolled aside, not quite ready to look at her face. He imagined it would be pale, her eyes glazed with fright.

"Rowan…" He cursed himself again. Every apology he could think of had less substance than air.

"Liam." She sighed it. When she shifted to curl against him, he pulled away abruptly, then rose to go to the window.

"Do you want water?"

"No." Her body continued to glow as she sat up. She didn't think to pull the sheets up as she usually did, but sat with them tangled around her legs. As she studied his stiff back, the glow began to fade. Doubts moved in.

"What did I do wrong?"

"What?" He glanced back. Her hair was a tangled mass of rich and gleaming brown around her shoulders, her body, so smooth and white, showed the marks of his hands, of the stubble he'd neglected to shave.

"I thought—well, but obviously I wasn't…I don't have any experience with what just happened here," she said with a faint edge to her voice. "If I did something wrong, or didn't do something you were expecting, the least you can do is tell me."

He could only stare. "Are you out of your mind?"

"I'm perfectly rational." So much so she wanted to bury her head in the pillow, pound her fists on the bed and weep. And scream. "Maybe I don't know a great deal about sex in practice, but I do know that without communication and honesty, that aspect of a relationship, as any other, is bound to fail."

"The woman's giving me a lecture," he murmured, dragging both hands through his hair. "At such a time she's giving me a lecture."

"Fine. Don't listen." Insulted, mortally wounded, she climbed out of bed. "You just stay there brooding out the window and I'll go home."

"You are home." He was nearly amused. "It's your cabin, your bedroom and your bed I just savaged you in."

"But—" Confused, and with the tattered remains of her shirt dangling from her hand, she focused. It was her bedroom, she realized. The big canopy bed stood between them, her lace curtains fluttered at the window where Liam stood, naked and irritable.

"Well then." She clutched her shirt and what was left of dignity. "You can go."

"You've a right to be angry."

"I certainly do." And she wasn't about to stand there having a crisis without any clothes on. She marched to the armoir and dragged out a robe.

"I'll apologize, Rowan, but it seems weightless after what I did to you. You had my word I wouldn't hurt you, and I broke it."

Unsure, she turned back, lifting the robe to her breasts rather than slipping it on. "Hurt me?"

"I wanted you, and I didn't think beyond that. Deliberately didn't think beyond it. I took what I pleased and I hurt you."

It wasn't annoyance in his eyes, she realized. It was guilt. And just one more wonder. "You didn't hurt me, Liam."

"There are marks on you I put there. You've tender flesh, Rowan, and I bruised it with carelessness. That I can fix easily enough, but—"

"Wait a minute, just a minute." She held up a hand

as he started forward. He stopped immediately, winced before he could prevent it.

"I don't mean to touch you but to take the bruises away."

"Just leave my bruises where they are." To give herself time to sort it out, she turned away and slipped on the robe. "You're upset because you wanted me."

"Because I wanted you enough to forget myself."

"Really?" She was smiling when she turned back and was thrilled to see his eyes narrow in what had to be confusion. "Well, I'm delighted. No one's ever wanted me enough for that. In my life no one's ever wanted me like that. I never imagined they could. My imagination isn't that...expansive," she decided.

It was she who stepped to him. "Now I don't have to imagine, because I know."

He combed his fingers through her hair before he realized he wanted to. Needed to. "I took your thoughts after you asked me not to."

"And gave me yours. Under these particular circumstances, I'm not complaining." She cupped her elbows, refused to be shy now. "What happened just now was thrilling. It was wonderful. You made me feel desired. Outrageously desired. The only thing that would hurt me is if you're sorry for it."

She was more than he'd understood, he realized. And her needs perhaps less...delicate. "Then I'm not a bit sorry." Still he took her hand, slid up the sleeve of her robe. "Let me take the bruises away. I don't want marks on you, Rowan. It matters to me."

He kissed her fingers, sending her heart into a long, slow flip. Then her lips, making it settle. As his lips rubbed gently on hers she felt the cool slide of something over her skin. The tiny aches she'd hardly noticed faded away.

"Will I get used to it, do you think?"

"To what?"

"Magic."

He wound a lock of her hair around his finger. "I don't know." *You would know,* a voice murmured in his head, *if you looked.*

"I've had a very magical day." She smiled. "I was going to see you when you...changed venues. I wanted to tell you that I met your father."

The finger in her hair stilled as his eyes whipped to hers. "My father?"

"I was sketching in the woods, and there he was. Well, the owl first, but I think I realized almost at once. I've seen him before," she added. "Once as an eagle. He wears a gold pendant always around his neck."

"Aye, he does." One that Liam had to accept or refuse.

"Then he—well, changed, and we talked. He's very handsome and very kind."

More than a little uneasy, Liam turned away to dress. "What did you speak of?"

"My sketches for the most part. He wanted one I'd done of you for your mother. I hope she likes it."

"That she will. She's partial to me."

She heard the affection in his voice and smiled. "He says she misses you—but I think he was speaking as much of himself. Actually I thought he might come to see you." Bottom lip caught between her teeth, she glanced at the tangled sheets of the bed. "It's a good thing he didn't, ah, drop in."

"He wouldn't be slipping into your bedroom for a visit," Liam said, and relieved now, grinned wickedly. "That's for me to do."

"But you'd like to see him, just the same."

"We keep in touch," he said, and found himself both amused and charmed as she walked over to tidy the bed. Wasting your time, Rowan Murray, for I'll be having you back in it before long.

"He's proud of you, and I think he liked me. He said—I probably shouldn't tell you."

"But you will." Liam tossed back his hair, moving to her as she plumped the pillows. "You've no guile at all."

"That's not such a bad thing." She nearly sulked, but felt too happy to bother. "He said I should ask you for something."

"Did he?" With a laugh, Liam sat on the bed. "And what will you, Rowan Murray? What should I conjure for you? A sapphire to go with your eyes? Diamonds to sparkle at your feet? If you want a boon from me, you've only to ask."

He grinned, fully amused now as she caught her bottom lip between her teeth once more. Women enjoyed baubles, he thought and began to wonder what sort he would give her.

"I'd like to meet more of your family." She blurted it out before she could change her mind.

He blinked twice. "My family?"

"Yes, well, I've met your father now, and Belinda—you said she was a relative, but I didn't know she was... Is she?''

''Aye.'' He said it absently, trying to realign his thoughts. ''You'd rather that than diamonds?''

''What would I do with diamonds? I suppose you think it's silly, but I'd just like to see how your family...lives.''

He considered, began to see the advantages and the path. ''It would make it easier for you to understand the magic, the life.''

''Yes, at least it seems it might. And I'm curious,'' she admitted. ''But if you'd rather not—''

He waved off her words. ''I've some cousins I haven't seen in some time.''

''In Ireland?''

''No, in California.'' He was too involved planning to note her quickly masked disappointment.

She had a craving to see Ireland.

''We'll pay them a visit,'' he decided, and rising held out a hand.

''Now?''

''Why not now?''

''Because I...'' She'd never expected him to agree or to move so quickly and could only look down help-lessly at her robe and bare feet. ''Well, I need to dress for one thing.''

With a delighted laugh, he grabbed her hand. ''Don't be foolish,'' he said and vanished them both.

Chapter 10

The next thing Rowan was absolutely sure of was standing with her arms locked like iron around Liam and her face pressed into his shoulder. Her heart was sprinting, her stomach jumping and there was the echo of rushing wind in her head.

"Beam me up, Scotty," was the best she could manage. And it made him roar with laughter.

"This is much simpler, and more enjoyable," he decided as he nudged her face up and indulged himself in a long, mind-numbing kiss.

"It has its points." Her voice had thickened, the way it did when she was stirred. It made Liam wonder if this impulsive trip might have been put off just a little while longer. As she loosened her grip, he kept his arms snug around her waist. "Where are we?"

"My cousin Morgana's garden. She kept one of the old family homes, raises her family here."

She jerked back, looked down and with a mixture of shock and relief noted her robe had been replaced by simple slacks and a shirt the color of ripening peaches.

She lifted a hand to her hair, found it still tousled. "I don't suppose I could have a brush."

"I like your hair this way," was his answer, as he drew her back so he could sniff it. "It's easier to get my hands into it."

"Hmm." As her system began to level, she could smell the flowers. Wild roses, heliotrope, lilies. She shifted and scanned the beams of sunlight, the cool pockets of shade. Arbors buried under triumphant blooms, sweeps of color, spears of shape with little stone paths winding through, seemingly at will.

"It's beautiful. Wonderful. Oh, I wish I knew how to make something as magical as this." She drew away to turn, to take in the trees sculpted by wind into bent, eerie shapes. Then she beamed as a gray wolf walked majestically down the path toward them. "Oh, is that—"

"A wolf," Liam said, anticipating her. "Not a relative. He's Morgana's." A child with dark hair and eyes as blue as lapis darted over the stones, then stopped with a keen and curious look in those striking eyes. "And so is he. Blessed be, cousin."

Liam felt the tug on his mind, stronger than he'd have expected from a boy no more than five, and lifted a brow. "It's rude to look so deep, or attempt to, without permission."

"You're in my garden," the boy said simply, but

his lips curved in a sweet smile. "You're cousin Liam."

"And you're Donovan. Blessed be, cousin." Liam stepped forward and offered a hand with great formality. "I've brought a friend. This is Rowan. And she prefers to keep her thoughts to herself."

Young Donovan Kirkland tilted his head, but minding his manners did no more than study her face. "She has good eyes. You can come in. Mama's in the kitchen."

Then the intense look faded from his face and he was just a normal little boy skipping ahead of them on the path with a dog prancing beside him, rushing to tell his mother they had company.

"He's a—he's a witch?" The full force of it struck her then. He was a child, astonishingly pretty with a missing front tooth, but he had power.

"Yes, of course. His father isn't, but blood runs strong in my family."

"I bet." Rowan let out a long breath. Witches or not, she thought, this was still a home and Liam hadn't bothered to, well, call ahead. "We shouldn't just…drop in like this on your cousin. She might be busy."

"We'll be welcome."

"It's just like a man to assume—" Then every thought ran out of her head as she caught her first glimpse of the house. It was tall, rambling, glinting in the sunlight. Towers and turrets speared up to that blue bowl that was the sky over Monterey. "Oh! It's like something out of a book. What a marvelous place to live."

Then the back door opened and Rowan was struck dumb with a combination of awe and pure female envy.

It was obvious where the boy got his looks. She'd never seen a more beautiful woman. Black hair cascaded over slim, strong shoulders, eyes of cobalt were heavily fringed by inky lashes. Her skin was creamy and smooth, her features fine and graceful. She stood, one hand on her son's shoulder, the other on the fierce head of the wolf while a large white cat ribboned between her legs.

And she smiled.

"Blessed be, cousin. You're welcome here." She moved to them, kissed Liam on both cheeks. "It's so good to see you. And you, Rowan."

"I hope we're not disturbing you," Rowan began.

"Family is always welcome. Come in, we'll have something cool to drink. Donovan, run up and tell your father we have company." As she spoke, she turned and gave her son a narrow glance. "Don't be lazy now. Go upstairs and tell him properly."

With a weary shrug of his shoulders, the boy dashed back in, shouting for his father.

"Well, close enough," Morgana murmured.

"He has a strong gift of sight."

"And he'll learn to use it well." Her voice took on the edge of an experienced and somewhat exasperated mother. "We'll have some iced tea," she said as they went into the large, airy kitchen. "Pan, sit."

"I don't mind him," Rowan said quickly, rubbing his ears as he sniffed at her. "He's gorgeous."

"I supposed you'd be used to handsome wolves,

wouldn't you.'' Sending Liam an amused look, she took out a clear pitcher filled with golden tea. ''It's still your favorite form, isn't it, Liam?''

''It suits me.''

''That it does.'' She glanced over as Donovan rushed in, side by side with his double.

''He's coming,'' Donovan said. ''He has to kill somebody first.''

''With a really big, sharp knife,'' said the twin, with relish.

''That's nice.'' After the absent comment, Morgana caught the look of shock on Rowan's face and laughed. ''Nash writes screenplays,'' she explained. ''He often murders gruesomely on paper.''

''Oh, yes.'' She accepted the glass of tea. ''Of course.''

''Can we have cookies?'' the twins wanted to know in unison.

''Yes. But sit down and behave.'' She only sighed as a tall glass jar filled with frosted cookies soared off the counter and landed on the table with a small crash and a wild wobble. ''Allysia, you'll wait until I serve our company.''

''Yes, ma'am.'' But she grinned mischievously as her brother giggled.

''I'll just sit, too...if you don't mind.'' Her legs had gone weak and Rowan dropped into a chair. ''I'm sorry, I just can't—I'm not really used to all this.''

''You're not...'' Morgana cut herself off, re-evaluating, and offered an easy smile. ''My children definitely take some getting used to.''

She reached for plates and opened her mind to her cousin. *You haven't told her yet, you dolt?*

It's my business. She's not ready.

Omission is kin to deceit.

I know what I'm doing. Serve your tea and cookies, Morgana, and let me handle this in my own way.

Stubborn mule.

Liam smiled a little, remembering she'd threatened to turn him into one during some scrap during their childhood. She might have managed it, he mused. She had a great deal of power in that particular area.

"I'm Ally, who are you?"

"I'm Rowan." Steadier, she smiled at the girl. A girl, she realized, she'd initially taken for a boy because of the scrappy little body and scraped knees. "I'm a friend of your cousin."

"You wouldn't remember me." Liam walked over to take a seat at the table. "But I remember you, young Allysia, and your brother, and the night you were born. In a storm it was, here in this house as your mother had been born in a storm in that same room. And in the hills of home there was starlight and singing to celebrate it."

"Sometimes we go to Ireland to visit Granda and Grandmama in our castle," Donovan told him. "One day I'll have a castle of my own on a high cliff by the sea."

"I hope you manage to figure out how to clean up your room first." This came from a man who stepped in with a rosy-cheeked girl tucked into each arm. "My husband, Nash, and our daughters, Eryn and

Moira. This is my cousin Liam, Nash, and his friend Rowan.''

''Nice to meet you. The girls woke up from their naps smelling cookies.''

He set the girls down. One toddled to the wolf who was sitting by the table hoping for crumbs. She fell adoringly on his neck. The other went directly to Rowan, crawled into her lap and kissed both of her cheeks much as her mother had kissed Liam in greeting.

Charmed, Rowan hugged her and rubbed a cheek on the soft golden hair. ''Oh, you have such beautiful children.''

Like, Liam thought as Moira settled cozily on Rowan's lap, often recognizes like.

''We've decided to keep them.'' Nash reached out to tickle the ribs of the older twins. ''Until something better comes along.''

''Daddy.'' Allysia sent him an adoring look, then nimbly snatched up her cookie before he could make the grab.

''You're quick.'' Nash tickled her again, and nipped the cookie out of her fingers. ''But I'm smarter.''

''Greedier,'' Morgana corrected. ''Mind your cookies, Rowan, he's not to be trusted around sweets.''

''What man is?'' Liam stole one from Rowan's plate and had Donovan snickering. ''How are Anastasia and Sebastian, their families?''

''You can judge for yourself,'' Morgana decided on the spot to invite her two cousins and their spouses

and families over. "We'll have a family cookout tonight to welcome you—and your friend."

Magic could be confusing, and it could be casual,
Rowan discovered. It could be stunning or as natural
as rain. Surrounded by the Donovans, flooded by the
scents from Morgana's garden, she began to believe
there could be little in this world that was more natural or more normal.

Morgana's husband, Nash, her cousin Sebastian
and Anastasia's husband, Boone, bickered over the
proper way to fire the grill. Ana sat comfortably in a
wicker chair nursing her infant son while her three
toddlers raced around the yard with the other children
and the dogs, all to the clashing sympathy of laughter,
shouts and wild barks.

At ease, Morgana nibbled on canapés and talked
lazily with Sebastian's wife, Mel—about children,
work, men, the weather, all the usual sorts of subjects
friends and family speak of on summer afternoons.

Rowan thought Liam held himself a bit aloof, and
wondered why. But when Ana's little sunshine-haired
daughter held up her arms to him she saw him smile,
pluck her up and fit her with casual skill on his hip.

She watched with some surprise as he walked with
her and apparently listened with great interest as she
babbled on to him.

He likes children, she realized, and the inner flutter
of longing nearly made her sigh.

This was a home, she thought. Whatever power
lived here, it was a home where children laughed and
squabbled, where they tumbled and whined just like

children everywhere. And men argued and talked of sports, women sat and spoke of babies.

And they were all so striking, she mused. Physically stunning. Morgana with her dazzling dark beauty, Anastasia so delicate and lovely, Mel sharp and sexy, her long body made only more compelling with its belly swollen with child.

Then the men. Just look at them, she thought. Gorgeous. Nash was dashing, golden, movie star handsome; Sebastian as romantic as a storybook prince with just an edge of wicked. And Boone tall and rugged.

And Liam, of course. Always Liam, dark and brooding with those wonderful flashes of amusement that glinted in his gold eyes.

Could she have stopped herself from falling in love with him? she wondered. No, not in a million years, not with all the power in heaven and earth in her hands.

"Ladies." Sebastian strolled over. Though he smiled at Rowan there was an intense look in his eyes that had her nerves dancing lightly. "The men require beer in order to accomplish such manly work."

Mel snorted. "Then you should be man enough to get it out of the cooler yourself."

"It's so much more fun being served." He stroked a hand over the slope of her belly. "She's restless," he murmured. "Do you want to lie down?"

"We're fine." She patted his hand. "Don't hover."

But when he leaned down, murmured something soft in her ear, her smile turned into a quiet glow.

"Get your beer, Donovan, and go play with your little friends."

"You know how excited I get when you insult me." He nipped her ear, making her laugh, before he plucked four bottles from the cooler and strolled off.

"The man gets mushy around babies," Mel commented, shifting herself so that she could reach the platter of finger food. "When Aiden was born Sebastian walked around as if he'd accomplished the whole deal by himself."

She watched their son wrap his arms around Sebastian's leg, then observed her elegant husband's limping, playful progress back to the men with Aiden in tow.

"He's a wonderful father." Ana lifted the heavy-eyed baby to her shoulder, gently rubbed his back. She smiled when her stepdaughter hurried over, glossy brown hair bouncing.

"Can I hold him now? I'll walk him until he's asleep then put him in the daybed in the shade. Please, Mama, I'll be careful."

"I know you will, Jessie. Here, take your brother."

Rowan watched, studying the girl of ten. Since she was Ana's stepdaughter and Boone wasn't…then neither was Jessie. Yet the girl didn't appear to feel out of place among her cousins. In fact, Rowan had seen her speak with the sharp impatience an older child often had for a younger one when Donovan had beaned her with a rubber ball.

"Would you like some wine, Rowan?" Without waiting for an answer, Morgana poured delicate straw-colored liquid into a glass.

"Thanks. It's so nice of you to have us here, to go to all this trouble without a bit of notice."

"It's our pleasure. Liam so rarely visits." Her eyes were warm and friendly as they met Rowan's. "Now why don't you tell us how you managed to get him here?"

"I just asked to meet some of his family."

"Just asked." Morgana exchanged a meaningful look with Ana. "Isn't that…interesting?"

"I hope you'll stay for a few days." Ana gave her cousin a warning pinch under the table. "I've kept my old house next door to where we live for family and friends when they visit. You're welcome to stay there."

"Thank you, but I didn't bring anything with me." She glanced down at the trim cotton blouse and slacks, reminding herself she'd left Oregon in nothing but a robe and had popped into Monterey neatly outfitted. "I suppose that doesn't matter, does it?"

"You'll get used to it." Mel laughed and bit into a carrot stick. "Mostly."

Rowan wasn't sure about that, but she did know she was comfortable here, with these people. Sipping her wine, she glanced over to where Liam stood with Sebastian. It was so nice for him, she thought, to have family to talk with, who understood and supported him.

"You're a moron," Sebastian said coolly.

"It's my business."

"So you always say." Tipping back his beer, Sebastian eyed his cousin out of amused gray eyes. "You don't change, Liam."

"Why should I?" He knew it was a childish response, but Sebastian often made him feel defensive and annoyed.

"What are you trying to accomplish? What do you need to prove? She's meant for you."

A chilly line he refused to recognize as fear snaked up Liam's spine. "It's still my decision."

Sebastian would have laughed, but he caught the flicker of unease in Liam's eyes, felt the shimmer of it in his mind. "More fool you," he murmured, but with some sympathy. "And if you feel that way, cousin, why haven't you told her?"

"I told her who I am." Liam spoke evenly, determined not to sound defensive. "Shown her. She nearly fainted." He remembered that moment, and the fury, the guilt he'd felt. "She's been raised not to believe."

"But she does believe. What she is has always been there. Until you tell her, she has no choice. And isn't choice your most prized possession?"

Liam studied Sebastian's smug smile with the active dislike only family could feel. When they'd been boys, Liam had competed ruthlessly against his older cousin, determined to be as fast, as clever, as smart. Under that competitive streak had been a secret layer of hero worship.

Even now, as a grown man, he wanted Sebastian's respect.

"When she's ready, she'll have the choice. And she'll make it."

"When *you're* ready," Sebastian corrected. "Is it arrogance, Liam, or fear?"

"It's sense," Liam shot back and fought not to let his teeth go on edge. "She's barely had time to absorb what I've told her already, much less to fully understand. Her own heritage is buried so deep there's hardly a glimmer of it in her mind. She's just begun to discover herself as a woman, how can I ask her to accept her gifts?"

Or me. But he didn't say that, infuriated himself that he would even think it.

He's in love with her, Sebastian realized as Liam turned to scowl down at the beach. In love and too hardheaded to admit it. For a second time a smile trembled on his lips with laughter just beneath. So the mighty fall, he mused, fighting all the way.

"It may be, Liam, you don't give the woman enough credit." He glanced back to where Rowan sat with his wife at the table. "She's lovely."

"She sees herself as plain, as simple. As ordinary. She's none of those things." Liam didn't look around. He could see her in his mind's eye clearly enough if he chose. "But she is tender. I may end up asking her for a great deal more than she's prepared to give."

Lovesick, Sebastian thought, though not without sympathy. He'd been similarly afflicted when he'd met Mel. And had very likely made similar stupid mistakes because of it.

"Living with you's more than any woman could be prepared for." He grinned when Liam turned his head and shot him a look with those hard gold eyes.

"I pity her at the thought of seeing that ugly, scowling face of yours day after day."

Liam's smile was sharp as a blade. "And how does your wife tolerate yours, cousin?"

"She's crazy about me."

"She strikes me as a smart woman."

"Her mind's like a dagger," Sebastian said, with a grinning glance at his wife.

"So how much time did it take you to weave the spell into her mind for that?"

This time Sebastian did laugh, and in a quick move grabbed Liam in a snug headlock. "A much shorter time than it'll take you to make your pretty lady believe you're a prize to look at."

"Kiss my—" He could only curse, struggle against laughter as Sebastian kissed him full on the mouth. "I'll have to kill you for that," he began, then lifted a brow as little Aiden dashed over to throw his arms around his father's legs. "Later," Liam decided and plucked the child up himself.

It was late when Liam left Rowan sleeping in the house Ana kept by the sea. He was restless, unsettled, and baffled by the ache around his heart that refused to ease.

He thought of running along the water, or flying over it. Racing until he was settled again.

And he thought of Rowan, sweetly sleeping in the quiet house.

He walked through the shadows and scents of Ana's garden, searching for peace of mind. He stepped through the hedge of faerie roses, crossed the lawn and stepped up on the deck on the house where Ana lived with her family.

He'd known she was there.

"You should be asleep."

Ana simply held out a hand. "I thought you'd want to talk."

But taking her hand, he sat beside her and contented himself with silence. He knew of no one more comfortable to sit with, to be with than Anastasia.

Overhead the moon winked in and out of clouds, the stars glimmered. The house where Rowan slept was dark and full of dreams.

"I didn't know how much I missed you, all of you, until I saw you again."

Ana gave his hand a supportive squeeze. "You needed to be alone for a while."

"Aye. It wasn't because you didn't matter that I blocked you all out for a time." He touched her hair. "It was because you did."

"I know that, Liam." She brushed her fingers over his cheek, felt his conflict in her own heart. "Your mind's so troubled." Her quiet gray eyes looked into his, her lips curved gently. "Must you always think so hard?"

"It's the only way I know." Still he felt the strain ease as he sat with her, sliding away knot by knot. That was Ana's gift. "You've a lovely family, Ana, and have made a lovely home here. Your mate is your match. Your children your joy. I can see how happy you are."

"Just as I can see how unhappy you are. Isn't a

family and a home what you want, Liam? What would make you happy?''

He studied their linked fingers, knowing he could and would say things to her he wouldn't to another. ''I might not be good at it.''

Ah, she realized, of course. Liam's standards for himself were always higher than anyone else's could be. ''What makes you think that?''

''I'm used to thinking for and of myself. Used to doing as I please. And I like it.'' He lifted his gaze to hers, smiled. ''I'm a selfish man, and fate's asking me to take the responsibility my father's borne so well, to take a woman who'll understand only pieces of what that means.''

''You're not giving either of you credit for who you are.'' There was impatience in her voice now, all the more effective as it was so rare. ''You've been stubborn, and you've been proud, but you've never been selfish, Liam. What you are is too bloody serious about too many things. And so you too often miss the joy of them.'' She sighed, shook her head. ''And Rowan can and will understand a great deal more than you seem to think.''

''I like going my own way.''

''And your own way led you straight to her, didn't it?'' This time Ana laughed. He looked so irritated that logic had turned back and nipped him. ''Do you know one of the things I've always admired most about you? Your instinct to question and pick apart everything. It's a fascinating and annoying trait. And you do it because you care so much. You'd rather not, but you care.''

"What would you do, Ana, if you were standing where I am?"

"Oh, that's easy for me." Her smoky eyes were soft, her smile gentle. "I'd listen to my heart. I always do. You'll do the same when you're ready."

"Not everyone's heart speaks as clearly as yours." Restless again, he drummed his fingers against the bench. "I've shown her who I am, but I haven't told her what that might mean to her. I've made her my lover, but I haven't given her love. I've shown her my family without telling her about her own. So yes, it troubles me."

"You can change it. It's in your hands."

He nodded, stared into the night. "I'm taking her back in the morning, when she wakes. And I'll show her what's sleeping inside her. As for the rest, I don't know yet."

"Don't only show her the obligations, Liam, the duties. Show her the joys, too." She rose, keeping her hand in his. "The baby's stirring. He'll be hungry. I'll make your goodbyes in the morning if you like."

"I'd appreciate it." He got to his feet, gathered her close. "Blessed be, cousin."

"Don't stay away so long." She kissed his cheeks before she drew away, and at the door paused, looked back. He stood in a shower of moonlight. Alone. "Love waits," she murmured.

It waited, Liam thought when he slipped into bed beside Rowan. Here, in dreams. Would it wait in the morning when he awakened her to all she was?

Like the princess in the fairy tale, he thought,

stirred to life by a kiss. The fact that he was, in his way, a prince made him smile humorlessly into the dark.

Fate, he supposed, enjoyed its ironies.

Those thoughts, and others, kept him awake and waiting for dawn. At first light he slipped a hand over hers, linked fingers and took them back to Rowan's own bed.

She murmured, shifted, then settled again. Rising, he dressed, studying her as she slept. Then he went quietly downstairs to make very strong coffee.

He thought both of them would need it.

With his mind tuned to hers, he knew the moment she stirred. He stepped outside, carrying his coffee. She would come to him, questioning.

Upstairs, Rowan blinked in puzzlement. Had she dreamed it all? It didn't seem possible when she could remember everything so clearly. The aching blue sky of Monterey, the bright music of children's laughter. The warmth of welcome.

It had to be real.

Then she let out a weak chuckle, resting her brow on her updrawn knees. Nothing had to be real, not anymore.

She rose, and prepared to experience yet another magical day.

Chapter 11

When she saw him standing on the porch, it struck her all over again. The wild thrill, the rush of love, the wonder. That this stunning, extraordinary man should want her left her speechless with delight.

Moving on pure emotion, she rushed through the door to throw her arms around him, press her cheek against that strong back.

It staggered him, those sweet, fresh feelings that poured out of her so freely, the quick rise of his own that tangled with them. He wanted to whirl around, to sweep her up and away to someplace where there was no one and nothing to think of but her.

Instead he laid his free hand over hers lightly.

"You brought us back before I had a chance to say goodbye to your family."

"You'll see them again…if you like."

"I would. I'd love to see Morgana's shop. It sounds

wonderful. And Sebastian and Mel's horses. I loved meeting all of your cousins.'' She rubbed her cheek over his shirt. "You're so lucky to have such a big family. I have some cousins on my father's side, but they live back east. I haven't seen them since I was a child.''

His eyes narrowed. Could there have been a more perfect opening for what he meant to tell her? "Go inside and get your coffee, Rowan. I need to talk to you.''

Her mood teetered as she loosened her grip, stepped back. She'd been so sure he'd turn and hold her. Instead he hadn't even looked at her, and his tone was cool.

What had she done wrong? she asked herself as she went inside to stare blindly at the line of cheerfully colored mugs. Had she said something? Not said something? Had she—

She squeezed her eyes shut, disgusted with herself. Why did she do that? she demanded. Why did she always, always assume she'd done something? Or lacked something?

Well, she wasn't going to do that anymore. Not with Liam. Not with anyone. A little grim, she got a mug and poured hot, black coffee to the rim.

When she turned, he was inside watching her. Ignoring the sudden dread in her stomach, she struggled to keep her voice impassive. "What do you want to talk to me about?''

"Sit down.''

"I'm fine standing.'' She pushed at her tumbled hair, sipped coffee hot enough to scorch her tongue.

"If you're angry with me, tell me. I don't like having to guess."

"I'm not angry with you. Why should I be?"

"I have no idea." To keep herself busy, she took out a loaf of bread to make toast she imagined would stick in her throat. "Why else would you be scowling at me?"

"I'm not scowling."

She glanced back at his face, sniffed in derision. "You certainly are, and I don't care for it."

His eyebrow shot up. Her mood had certainly shifted from soft and cuddly to cold and snappy quickly. "Well, I beg your pardon then." In an irritable move, he yanked out a chair, straddled it.

Get on with it, he ordered himself.

"I took you to meet my family, and it's family I want to speak of. I'd prefer it if you'd sit the bloody hell down instead of prowling about the room."

Her shoulders wanted to hitch up in defense at the angry tone and she forced them to stay straight. "I'm making breakfast, if you don't mind."

He muttered something, then flung out his hands. A plate of lightly browned toast appeared on the counter. "There. Though how you can call that breakfast is beyond me. Now sit down with it."

"I'm perfectly capable of making my own." But she carried the plate to the table before deliberately going to the refrigerator and taking her own sweet time choosing jam.

"Rowan, you're trying my patience. I'm only asking you to sit down and talk to me."

"Asking is exactly what you didn't do, but now

that you have, I will.'' Surprised at just how smug she felt over that small victory, she came back to the table and sat down. "Do you want some toast?''

"No, I don't.'' And hearing the snap in his voice, sighed. "Thank you.''

She smiled at him with such sudden, such open sweetness, his heart stumbled. "I hardly ever win arguments,'' she told him as she spread jam on the toast. "Especially when I don't know what the argument's about.''

"Well, you won that one, didn't you?''

Her eyes danced as she bit into the toast. "I like winning.''

He had to laugh. "So do I.'' He laid a hand on her wrist as she lifted her mug. "You didn't add your cream and all that sugar. You know you don't like your coffee black.''

"Only because I make lousy coffee. Yours is good. You said you wanted to talk about your family.''

"About family.'' He moved his hand so he was no longer touching her. "You understand what runs through mine.''

"Yes.'' He was watching her so closely, his eyes so focused on hers she had to fight the urge to squirm. "Your gift. The Donovan Legacy.'' She smiled. "That's what you named your company.''

"Aye, that's right. Because I'm proud of where I come from. Power has obligations, responsibilities. It's not a toy, but it's not something to fear.''

"I'm not afraid of you, Liam, if that's what worries you.''

"Maybe, in part.''

"I'm not, I couldn't be." She wanted to reach out to him, to tell him she loved him, but he pushed back from the table and began to prowl about the room just as he'd asked her not to.

"You're seeing it as a storybook. Magic and romance and happy-ever-after. But it's just life, Rowan, with all its messes and mistakes. Its needs and demands. Life," he repeated, turning back to her, "that has to be lived."

"You're only half right," she told him. "I can't help but see it as magical, as romantic, but I understand the rest. How could I not understand after meeting your cousins, seeing their families? That's what I met yesterday, a family. Not a picture in a book."

"And you were...comfortable with them?"

"Very much." Her heart began to trip in her throat. It mattered to him, she could see it. Mattered that she accepted his family, and him. Because...was it possible it was because he loved her, too? That he wanted her to be part of his life?

Joy spurted through her in one long liquid gush.

"Rowan." He came back to sit, so that she hid her trembling hands under the table. "My cousins are many. Here, in Ireland. In Wales, Cornwall. Some are Donovans, some Malones, some Rileys. And some are O'Mearas."

Her heart had bounded into her head to spin dreamily. "Yes, you said your mother was an O'Meara. We might even be distant relatives. Wouldn't that be nice? Then in some convoluted way I might be connected to Morgana and the rest."

He bit back a sigh, then reaching for her hands, he

took them firmly in his and leaned closer. "Rowan, I didn't say we might be cousins, but that we *are* cousins. Distant, it's true, but we share blood. A legacy."

Puzzled by the sudden intensity she frowned at him. "I suppose we might be. Tenth cousins or something, however many times removed. I'm not entirely clear how that works. It's interesting, but…"

This time her heart seemed to stop. "What do you mean?" she said slowly. "We share a legacy?"

"Your great-grandmother, Rowan O'Meara was a witch. As I am. As you are."

"That's absurd." She started to jerk her hands free, but he held them fast. "That's absurd, Liam. I didn't even know her, and you certainly didn't."

"I know of her." He spoke calmly now. "Of Rowan O'Meara from Clare, who fell in love and married, and left her homeland, and abjured her gifts. She did this because the man she loved asked it of her. She did this freely, as was her right. And when she birthed her children, she said nothing of their heritage until they were grown."

"You're thinking of someone else," was all she could say.

"So they thought her eccentric, and perhaps a bit fey, but they didn't believe. When they birthed children of their own, they only said Rowan O'Meara was odd. Kind and loving, but odd. And when the daughter of her daughter birthed a daughter, that child was raised not knowing what ran in her blood."

"A person would have to know. How could you not know?" This time he released her hands so she could pull back, spring to her feet. "You'd feel it. You'd sense it."

"And haven't you?" He got to his feet as well, wishing he'd found a way to tell her without frightening her. "Haven't you felt it, from time to time? Felt that stirring, that burn in the blood, wondered at it?"

"No." That was a lie, she thought and backed away. "I don't know. But you're wrong, Liam. I'm just ordinary."

"You saw pictures in the flames, dreamed your dreams as a child. Felt the tingle of power under your skin, in your mind."

"Imagination," she insisted. "Children have wonderful ones." But she felt a tingle now, and part of it was fear.

"You said you weren't afraid of me." He said it softly, as he might to a deer startled in the woods. "Why would you be afraid of yourself?"

"I'm not afraid. I just know it's not true."

"Then you'd be willing to test it, to see which of us is right?"

"Test what? How?"

"The first skill learned and the last to leave is the making of fire. What's inside you already knows how it's done. I'll just remind you." He stepped to her, taking her hand before she could evade. "And you have my word that I won't do it myself, just as I want your word that you won't block what comes."

It seemed even her soul was trembling now. "I don't have to block anything because there isn't anything."

"Then come with me."

"Where?" she demanded as he pulled her outside. But she already knew.

"The dance," he said simply. "You won't have control just yet, and it's protected."

"Liam, this is ridiculous. I'm just a normal woman, and in order to make a fire I need kindling and a match."

He paused just long enough to glare at her. "You think I'm lying to you?"

"I think you're mistaken." She had to scramble to keep up with his ground-eating strides. "There probably was a Rowan O'Meara who was a witch. There probably was, Liam, but she wasn't my great-grandmother. My great-grandmother was a sweet, slightly dotty old woman who painted beautifully and told fairy stories."

"Dotty?" The insult of that brought him up short. "Who told you that?"

"My mother—that is—"

"So." He nodded as if she'd just confirmed everything he'd said. "Dotty," he muttered as he began to stride along again. "The woman gives up everything for love and they call her dotty. Aye, maybe she was at that. She'd have been better off staying in Ireland and mating with one of her own."

Then he wouldn't be stalking down this path with Rowan's trembling hand in his, he thought.

He wasn't entirely sure if he was pleased or annoyed with that particular twist of fate.

When he reached the stone circle, he pulled her directly to the center. She was out of breath, from the quick walk and from what she could feel swimming in the air.

"The circle's cast and so it begins. I ask that all be safe within. This woman comes that she may see. As I will, so mote it be."

As the chant ended, the wind swept through the stones, wrapped like a warm caress around Rowan's body. Startled, she crossed her arms over her breasts, gripped her own shoulders. "Liam—"

"You should be calm, but that will be hard for you. Nothing here will harm you, Rowan, I swear to you." He laid his hands over hers and kissed her, gently but deeply, until the stiffness of her body softened. "If you won't trust yourself, trust me."

"I do trust you, but this—I'm afraid of this."

He stroked a hand down her hair, and realized in many ways what he was doing was like initiating a virgin to love. It should be done sweetly, patiently, and with thoughts only on her.

"Think of it as a game." He smiled at her as he stepped back. "A more basic one than you imagine just now." He drew her down to her knees. "Breathe deep and slow until you hear your heartbeat in your head. Close your eyes if it helps, until you're steady."

"You tell me I'm going to make fire out of nothing, and then ask me to be steady." But she closed her eyes. The sooner she could prove to him he was mistaken, the sooner it would be over.

"A game," she said on the first long breath. "All right, just a game, and when you see I'm no good at it, we'll go home and finish breakfast."

Remember what you weren't told, but knew. Liam's

voice was a quiet murmur inside her mind. *Feel what you always felt but never understood. Listen to your heart. Trust your blood.*

"Open your eyes, Rowan."

She wondered if this was like being hypnotized. To be so fully, almost painfully aware, yet to be somehow outside yourself. She opened her eyes, looked into his as sunlight streamed between them. "I don't know what to do."

"Don't you?" There was the faintest lilt of amusement in his voice now. "Open yourself, Rowan. Believe in yourself, accept the gift that's been waiting for you."

A game, she thought again. Just a game. In it she was a hereditary witch, with power sleeping just under the surface. Waking it was only a matter of believing, of wanting, of accepting.

She stretched out her hands, stared at them as if they belonged to someone else who watched them tremble lightly. They were narrow hands, with long slender fingers. Ringless, strangely elegant. They cast twin shadows on the ground.

She heard her own heartbeat, just as he'd told her. And she heard the slow, deep sound of her own breathing, as if she were awake listening to herself sleep.

Fire, she thought. For light, for heat. For comfort. She could see it in her mind, pale gold flames just touched with deep red at the edges. Glowing low and simmering, rising up like torches to the sky. Smokeless and beautiful.

Fire, she thought again, for heat, for light. Fire that burns both day and night.

Dizzy, she swayed a little. Liam had to fight every instinct to keep from reaching out to her.

Then her head fell back, her eyes went violently blue. The air hushed. Waited. He watched as she lost a kind of innocence.

Power whipped through her like the wind that suddenly rose to send her hair flying. The sudden heat of it made her gasp, made her shudder. Then it streaked like a rocket down her arms, seemed to shoot from her fingers into a pool of light.

She saw with dazzled eyes, the fire she'd made.

It sizzled on the ground, tiny dancing flames of gold edged with red. The heat of it warmed her knees, then her hands as she hesitantly stretched them over it. As she drew them back, the flames shot high.

"Oh. Oh, no!"

"Ease back, Rowan. You need a bit of control yet."

He brought the thin column of fire down as she stared and stuttered.

"How did I—how could I—" She snapped her gaze to his. "You."

"You know it wasn't me. It's your heritage, Rowan, and your choice whether you accept it or not."

"It came from me." She closed her eyes, inhaling, exhaling slowly until she could do so without her breath shuddering out. "It came from me," she repeated, and looked at him. She couldn't deny it now, what some part of her knew. Perhaps had always known.

"I felt it, I saw it. There were words in my head, like a chant. I don't know what to think, or what to do."

"What do you feel?"

"Amazed." She let out a dazed laugh and stared at her own hands. "Thrilled. Terrified and delighted and wonderful. There's magic in me." It shimmered in her eyes, glowed on her face. This time her laugh was full and free as she sprang up to turn circles inside the ring of stones.

Grinning widely, Liam sat with his legs crossed and watched her embrace self-discovery. It made her beautiful, he realized. This sense of sheer joy gave her a rich and textured beauty.

"All my life I've been average. Pathetically ordinary, tediously normal." She spun another circle then collapsed on the ground beside him to throw her arms around his neck. "Now there's magic in me."

"There always was."

She felt like a child with hundreds and hundreds of brightly wrapped presents waiting to be opened and explored. "You can teach me more."

"Aye." Understanding something of what was racing through her, he flicked a finger down her cheek. "I can. I will. But not just now. We've been here more than an hour, and I want my breakfast."

"An hour." She blinked as he rose and hauled her to her feet. "It seems like just a few minutes."

"It took you a while to get down to things. It won't take you so long the next time." With a thought he put out the fire. "We'll see if we can find where your talents lie once I've had my meal."

"Liam." She turned into him for a moment, pressed her lips to his throat. "Thank you."

She learned fast. Liam had never considered himself a good teacher, but he supposed it had something to do with the student.

This one was open and eager and quick.

It didn't take long to determine her talents channeled into magic, as Morgana's did. Within a day or two, they determined she had no real gift for seeing. She could give him her thoughts, but could only read his clearly if he put them into her head.

And while she couldn't, even after more than an hour of sweaty concentration, transform herself, she turned a footstool into a rosebush with laughing delight.

Show her the joy, Ana had told him. But he understood she was showing *him* as she danced around the clearing, turning the early summer flowers into a maze of color and shape. Rocks became jewel-colored crystals, infant blooms exploded into huge fireworks of brilliant hues. The little stream rose into an elegant waterfall of luminous blue.

He didn't rein her in. She deserved to ride on the wonder of it. Responsibilities, choices, he knew, would come soon enough.

She was creating her own fairy tale. It was so easy all at once to see it perfectly in her mind. And in seeing it, to make it real. Here was her little cottage in the forest, with the stunning witch garden spread out, the sweep of water rising, the whip of the wind blowing free.

And the man.

She turned, unaware how devastating she looked just then with her hair streaming, glossy and wild, her arms flung out and the light of young power in her eyes.

"Just for today. I know it can't stay like this, but just for today. I used to dream of being in a place just like this, with water and wind rushing, and flowers so huge and bright they dazzled your eyes. And the scent of them…"

She trailed off, realizing she had dreamed of this, exactly this. And of him, of Liam Donovan stepping off the porch of a pretty cottage and moving to her, walking under an arbor of flowers that rained pretty pink petals onto the ground.

He would pluck a rose, white as a snowflake from a bush as tall as he. And offer it to her.

"I dreamed," she said again. "When I was a little girl."

He plucked a rose, white as a snowflake from a bush as tall as he. And offered it to her. "What did you dream, Rowan Murray?"

"Of this." Of you. So often of you.

"Just for today, you can have your dream."

She sighed as she traced the rose down her cheek. Just for today, she thought, would be enough. "I was wearing a long blue dress. A robe, really. And yours was black, with gold edgings." She laughed, enchanted as she felt the thin silk caress her skin. "Did I do that, or did you?"

"Does it matter? It's your dream, Rowan, but I'm hoping I kissed you in it."

"Yes." She sighed again as she moved into his arms. "The kind of kiss dreams are made on."

He touched his lips to hers, softly at first. Warming them, softening them, until they parted on a quiet breath. Then deeper, slowly deeper while her arms came up to circle him, while her fingers slipped lazily into his hair.

As he did something trembled in his memory as well. Something once seen or once wished for. When he gave himself to it, he began to float in dreams with her. And so drew her closer.

Together they circled, a graceful dance with hearts keeping the beat.

Her feet no longer touched the ground as they spun. The dreams of a romantic young girl shimmered and shaped into the needs of a woman. Warmth skimmed over her skin as she held him tighter, drew him into her heart. As she offered him more. Offered him everything.

There were candles in her dream. Dozens of them, fragrant and white and burning in tall silver stands with gilded leaves winding around them. And a bed, lit by them, draped in white and gold.

When he carried her to it, she was dizzy with love, washed in wonder.

"How could I have known?" She drew him down to her. "How could I have forgotten?"

He wondered the same of himself, but couldn't question it now, not now when she was so soft, so giving, when her lips were parting for his and her sigh of pleasure slipped into him like wine from a golden cup.

The sun dipped down behind the trees, edging them with fire, shooting color into the deepening sky. In the trees, the birds sang to those last lights.

"You're beautiful."

She wouldn't have believed it. But here, now, she felt beautiful. She felt powerful. She felt loved. Just for today, she thought and met his mouth with hers.

He drank from her, with thirst but without greed. Held her close but without desperation. Here, they both knew, time could spin out. Time could be taken.

Tongues met and tangled in a slow, intimate dance. Breath mixed. Murmurs melded.

She stroked her hands along the silk of his robe, then beneath to flesh. So warm. So smooth. His mouth on her throat, urging her to tip her head to give him more, and the light nip of teeth where her pulse beat. The erratic bump of it tempted him to slick his tongue over her skin, to fill himself with the flavor that was only her.

He parted her robe, lightly as air. When his hands, his mouth took possession of her, she arched gently.

Enjoy me, she seemed to say. Enchant me.

She sighed with him, moved with him, while the air swam with scent and the warm, soft wind caressed her naked skin. Sensations glimmered, tangled with delights both bright and dark. Lost in them, steeped in them, she rolled with him, rose languidly over him.

Her body was wand slim, white as marble in the delicate light. Her hair was lifted by the wind, her eyes full of secrets. Captivated, he ran his hands up her thighs, over her hips, her torso, closed them over her breasts.

And there her heart beat in the same hammer blows as his own.

"Rowan," he murmured, as those secrets, as that power glinted in her eyes. "You are all manner of witch."

Her laugh was quick and triumphant. She leaned down, took his mouth hungrily with hers. Heat, sudden and brutal slammed into him, leaped into his blood like the fire she'd made only hours before.

She felt it, too, the quick change, and that she had made it. That, she thought wildly, that was power. Riding on it she took him into her, bowing back to revel in the shock of it, watching stars wheel in the black sky overhead.

His hands gripped her hips, his breath exploded from his lungs. Instinctively he struggled for control, but his already slippery grasp broke as she took him.

She took. Her hips moved like lightning, her body soared with a wild whip of energy that pushed him, raced ahead, dragged him with her.

She rocked herself to madness, then beyond, and still she drove him on. He said her name. She heard the sound break from him as his body plunged with hers. And she saw as they flew up, how his eyes flashed, then went dark and blind.

She all but wept with triumph as she grabbed hold and fell over with him.

He'd never allowed a woman to take control. Now, as Rowan lay sprawled over him, he realized he hadn't been able to stop it. Not with her. There were a great many things he hadn't been able to stop with her.

He turned his face into her hair and wondered what would come next. Only seconds later, when she spoke, he knew.

"I love you, Liam." She said it quietly, with her lips over his heart. "I love you."

He called the panic that sprang up inside him sense, responsibility. "Rowan—"

"You don't have to love me back. I just can't stand not telling you anymore. I was afraid to tell you before." She shifted, looked at him. "I don't think I'll be afraid of anything ever again. So I love you, Liam."

He sat up beside her. "You don't know all there is to know, so you can't know what you think or what you feel. Or what you'll want," he added on a huff of breath. "I have things to explain, things to show you. We'll do better at my cabin."

"All right." She made her smile easy, even as a dread filled her heart that the magic of that day was over.

Chapter 12

What else could he tell her that would shock or surprise? Rowan asked herself. He'd told her he was a witch, then had proved it and somehow made her accept it. He'd wiped out twenty-seven years of her simple beliefs about herself by telling her she was a witch as well. Had proved it. She had not only accepted it, but had embraced it.

How much more could there be?

She wished he would speak. But he said nothing as they walked through moonlight from her cabin to his. She'd known him long enough to understand when he fell into this kind of silence he would tell her nothing until he was ready.

By the time they reached his cabin and stepped inside her nerves were strung tight.

What she didn't think about, refused to consider,

was the fact that he'd withdrawn into that silence after she'd told him she loved him.

"Is it so serious?" She tried for a light tone but the words came out uneven, and very close to a plea.

"For me, yes. You'll decide what it means to you."

He moved into the bedroom and running his fingers over the wall beside the fireplace opened a door she hadn't known was there into a room she'd have sworn didn't exist.

A soft light glowed from it, as pale and cool as the moonlight.

"A secret room?"

"Not secret," he corrected. "Private. Come in, Rowan."

It was a measure of her trust in him that she stepped forward into that light. The floor was stone, smooth as a mirror, the walls and ceiling of wood, highly polished. Light and the shadow she cast reflected back off those surfaces and shimmered like water.

There was a table, richly carved and inlaid, and on it a bowl of thick blue glass, a stemmed cup of pewter, a small mirror with a silver back ornately scrolled and a slim, smooth handle of amethyst. Another bowl held small, colorful crystals. A round globe of smoky quartz stood on the silver backs of a trio of winged dragons.

What did he see when he looked into it? she wondered. What would she see?

But she turned and watched Liam light candles, watched their flames rise into air already perfumed with fragrant smoke.

She saw another table then, a small round surface on a simple pedestal. Liam opened the box resting there, took out a silver amulet on a chain. He held it a moment, as if testing its weight, then set it down with a quiet jingle of metal on wood.

"Is this…a ceremony?"

He glanced over, those tawny eyes distracted as if he'd forgotten she was there. But he hadn't forgotten her. He'd forgotten nothing.

"No. You've had a lot to deal with, haven't you, Rowan? You've asked me not to touch your thoughts so I can't know what's in your mind, how you're thinking of all this."

He hadn't meant to touch her, but found his fingers grazing her cheek. "A lot of it I can read in your eyes."

"I've told you what I think and what I feel."

"So you have."

But you haven't told me, she thought, and because it hurt her, she turned away. "Will you explain to me what everything is for?" she asked and traced a fingertip over the scrolling on the little mirror.

"Tools. Just pretty tools," he told her. "You'll need some of your own."

"Do you see things in the glass?"

"Aye."

"Are you ever afraid to look?" She smiled a little and looked back at him. "I think I might be."

"What's seen is…possibility."

She wandered, avoiding him. There was change coming. Whether it was her woman's instincts or her newly discovered gifts that told her, she was sure of it. In a glass case were more stones, stunning clusters with spears rising, smooth towers, jewel-tone globes.

He waited her out, not with patience but because for once he didn't know how to begin. When she turned back to him, her hands linked nervously, her eyes full of doubts, he had no choice but to choose.

"I knew you were coming here."

He didn't mean here, to this room, tonight. He saw her acknowledge this. "Did you know...what would happen?"

"Possibilities. There are always choices. We each made ours, and have more to make yet. You know something of your heritage and of mine, but not all. In my country, in my family, there is a tradition. It's simplest, I suppose, to compare it to rank, though it's not precisely that. But one takes a place as head of the family. To guide, and counsel. To help in settling disputes should they arise."

Once again he picked up the silver amulet, once again he set it down.

"Your father wears one of those in gold."

"Aye, he does."

"Because he's head of the family?"

She was quick, Liam thought. Foolish of him to have forgotten that. "He is, until he chooses to pass on the duty."

"To you."

"It's traditional for the amulet to be passed down to the oldest child. But there are choices, on both sides, and there are...stipulations. To inherit, one must be worthy of it."

"Of course you are."

"One must want it."

Her smile faded into a look of puzzlement. "Don't you?"

"I haven't decided." He slipped his hands into his pockets before he could pick up the amulet again. "I came here to take time, to think and consider. It must be my choice. I won't be bullied by fate."

The regal tone of his voice made her smile again. "No, you wouldn't be. That's another reason you'd be good at it." She started to go to him, but he held up a hand.

"There are other requirements. If there is marriage, it must be to a mate with elfin blood, and the marriage must be for love, not for duty. Both must enter into it freely."

"That seems only right," she began, then stopped. As Liam had said, she was quick. "I have elfin blood, and I've just told you I'm in love with you."

"And if I take you, my choices diminish."

This time it took her a moment. It had been said so coolly it was like an iced sword to the heart. "Your choices, I see." She nodded slowly while inside she fought to save the scattered pieces of her heart, the pitiful tatters of her pride. "And your choices include accepting this aspect of your heritage or abjuring it. You'd take that very, very seriously, wouldn't you, Liam?"

"How could I not?"

"And I'm more or less like a weight for the scale. You just have to decide which bowl to set me in. How...awkward for you."

"It's not as simple as that," he shot back, off balance by her sudden sharp tones. "It's my life."

"And mine," she added. "You said you knew I was coming here, but I didn't know about you. So I had no choice there. I fell in love with you the minute I saw you, but you were prepared and you had your own agenda. You *knew* I would love you."

It was hurled at him, a bitter accusation that had him staring at her. "You're mistaken."

"Oh, really? How many times did you slip into my mind to see? Or come into my house as a wolf and listen to me babble? Without giving me the choice you're so damn fond of. You knew I met the requirements, so you studied and measured and considered."

"I didn't know!" He shouted it at her, furious to have his actions tilted toward deceit. "I didn't know until you told me about your great-grandmother."

"I see. So up to that point you were either playing with me or deciding if you could use me as your out should you decide to refuse your position."

"That's ridiculous."

"Then suddenly you've got a witch on your hands. You wanted her—I don't doubt you wanted me, and I was pathetically easy. I took whatever you chose to give me, and was grateful."

It humiliated her to think of it now, to remember how she had rushed into his arms, trusting her heart. Trusting him.

"I cared for you, Rowan. I care for you."

Her cheeks were ghost pale in the flickering light, her eyes dark and deep. "Do you know how insulting that is? Do you know how humiliating it is to understand that you knew I was in love with you while you figured the angles and made your choices? What choice did I have, what choice did you give me?"

"All I could."

She shook her head fiercely. "No, all you *would*," she tossed back. "You knew exactly how vulnerable I was when I came here, how lost."

"I did, yes. That's why I—"

"So you offer me a chance to work with you," she interrupted. "Knowing I was already dazzled by you, knowing how desperately I needed something. Then, in your own good time, you told me who you were, who I was. At your pace, Liam, always at your pace. And each time I moved exactly as you expected I would. It's all been just another game."

"That's not true." Incensed, he took her arms. "I thought of you, too damn much of you. And did what I thought was right, what was best."

The jolt shot through his fingertips, up his arms, with such heat and power, it knocked him back a full two steps. This time he could only gape at her, shocked to the core that she'd caught him so completely unaware.

"Damn it, Rowan." His hands still stung from the slap of her will.

"I won't be bullied, either." Her knees were jellied at the realization she'd had not only the ability but the fury to shove him back with her mind. "This isn't what you expected, this isn't one of your possibilities. I was supposed to come in here with you tonight, listen to you, then fold my hands, bow my head like the quiet little mouse I am, and leave it all up to you."

Her eyes were vividly blue, her face no longer pale but flushed with anger, and to his annoyance outrageously beautiful. "Not precisely," he said with dignity. "But it is up to me."

"The hell it is. You have to decide what you want, true enough, but don't expect me to sit meekly while you choose or discard me. Always, always, people have made decisions for me, chosen the way my life should go. What have you done but the same?"

"I'm not your parents," he shot back. "Or your Alan. These were different circumstances entirely."

"Whatever the circumstances, you held the controls and guided me along. I won't tolerate that. I've been ordinary." The words ripped out of her, straight from the belly. "You wouldn't understand that, you've never been ordinary. But I have, all my life. I won't be ordinary again."

"Rowan." He would try calm, he told himself. He would try reason. "All I wanted for you was what you wanted for yourself."

"And what I wanted most, was for you to love me. Just me, Liam, whatever and however I am. I didn't let myself expect it, but I wanted it. My mistake was in still not thinking enough of myself."

Tears shone in her eyes now, unmanning him. "Don't weep. Rowan, I never meant to hurt you." He took her hand now, and she let it lay limply in his.

"No, I'm sure you didn't," she said quietly. The force of her fury had passed. Now she was only tired. "That only makes it sadder. And me more pathetic. I told you I loved you." Tears still trembled on the edge of her voice. "And you know I do. But you can't tell me, you can't decide if it…suits you."

She swallowed the tears, reached deep for the pride she'd used too rarely. "From here, I decide my own fate." She drew her hand from him, stood back. "And you yours."

She turned to the door, bringing him a fresh and baffling wave of panic. "Where are you going?"

"Where I please." She glanced back. "I was your lover, Liam, but never your partner. I won't settle for that, not even for you." She let out a quiet breath, studying him in the shifting light. "You had my heart in your hands," she murmured. "And you didn't know what to do with it. I can tell you, without the crystal ball, without the gift, you'll never have another like it."

As she slipped away from him he knew it was not only prophecy, it was truth.

It took her a week to deal with the practicalities. San Francisco hadn't changed in the months she'd been gone, nor in the days she'd been back. But she had.

She could look out her window now, at the city and realize it hadn't been the place that had dissatisfied her, but her place in it. It was doubtful she'd ever live there again, but she thought she could look back and find memories—good and bad. Life was made up of both.

"Are you sure you're doing the right thing, Rowan?" Belinda asked. She was a graceful woman, with dark hair, short as a pixie's, and eyes of misty green.

Rowan glanced up from her packing and looked into Belinda's concerned face. "No, but I'm doing it just the same."

Rowan had changed, Belinda mused. She was certainly stronger, more than a little wounded. Guilt nagged at her. "I feel some responsibility in this."

"No." Rowan said it firmly, and smoothed a sweater into her suitcase. "You're not responsible."

Restless, Belinda wandered to the window. The bedroom was nearly empty now. She knew Rowan had given many of her things away, stored others. In the morning, she would be gone. "I sent you there."

"No, I asked if I could use your cabin."

Belinda turned. "There were things I could have told you."

"You weren't meant to—I understand that, Belinda."

"If I'd known Liam would be such a jackass, I—" She broke off, scowled. "I should have, I've known him all my life. A more stubborn, thickheaded, irritating man has yet to be born." Then she sighed. "But he's kind with it, and most of his stubbornness comes from caring so much."

"You don't have to explain him to me. If he'd trusted me, believed in me, things might be different." She took the last of her clothes from the closet, laid them on the bed. "If he'd loved me, everything would be different."

"Are you so sure he doesn't?"

"I've decided the only thing I can be sure of is

myself. It was the hardest and most valuable thing I learned while I was away. Do you want this blouse? It never flattered me.''

''It's more my color than yours.'' Belinda wandered over, laid a hand on Rowan's shoulder. ''Did you speak with your parents?''

''Yes. Well, I tried.'' Thoughtfully Rowan folded trousers, packed them. ''On one level it went better than I ever expected. They were upset at first, and baffled, that I'm going away, that I'm giving up teaching. Naturally, they tried to point out the flaws, the consequences.''

''Naturally,'' Belinda repeated, just dryly enough to make Rowan smile.

''They can't help it. But we talked a long time. You know, I don't think we've actually talked like that before. I explained why I was going, what I wanted to do and why—well not all the why.''

''You didn't ask your mother about what you are?''

''In the end, I couldn't. I mentioned my grandmother, and legacies, and how being named after her had turned out to be so...appropriate. My mother waved it off. No,'' Rowan corrected with a sigh, ''closed it off. It's as if she'd blocked it off—if she ever even really knew or suspected. What runs through my blood, and even through her own, simply doesn't exist in her world.''

''So you left it at that?''

''Why should I push her on something that makes her uncomfortable or unhappy?'' Rowan lifted her hands. ''I'm content with it, so that's enough. If I'd insisted on stripping away whatever barrier she'd put up, what purpose would it serve?''

"None. You did the right thing, for yourself and your mother.''

"What matters is, in the end, my parents understood as much as they're able about the decisions I've made. Because in the end all they want is for me to be happy.''

"They love you.''

"Yes, maybe more than I ever gave them credit for.'' And she smiled. "It helps some that Alan's been seeing someone else—a math instructor. My mother finally broke down and told me she's had them over for dinner and they're charming together.''

"We'll wish them well.''

"I wish them very well. He's a nice man and deserves to be happy.''

"So do you.''

"Yes, you're right.'' Giving it one last look, Rowan closed the last suitcase. "I intend to be. I'm excited, Belinda, nervous, but excited. Going to Ireland like this. One way ticket.'' She pressed a hand to her uneasy stomach. "Not knowing if I'll stay or where I'll go or what I'll do. It's thrilling.''

"You'll go first to Castle Donovan in Clare? See Morgan's and Sebastian's and Ana's parents?''

"Yes. I appreciate you contacting them, and their asking me to stay.''

"You'll enjoy them, and they you.''

"I hope so. And I want to learn more.'' Rowan stared into the middle distance. "I very much want to learn.''

"Then you will. Oh, I'll miss you. Cousin." With this Belinda caught Rowan in a hard embrace. "I have to go, before I start blubbering. Call me," she ordered, scooping up the blouse as she hurried out of the room. "Write, whistle in the wind, but keep in touch."

"I will." Rowan walked her to the door of the empty apartment, exchanged one last fierce hug. "Wish me luck."

"That and more. Blessed be, Rowan." Already sniffling, she dashed out.

Weepy herself, Rowan closed the door, turned and looked. There was nothing left here, she thought. Nothing left to do. She'd be moving on in the morning. Moving in a way she'd never imagined. She had family in Ireland, and roots. It was time to explore them, and in doing so, to explore herself.

What she'd already learned gave her the foundation to build more.

And if she thought of Liam, if she pined for him, so be it. She could live with heartache, but she couldn't—wouldn't live with distrust.

The knock on the door surprised her, then she smiled. Belinda, she imagined, not quite ready to say goodbye.

But the woman at the door was a stranger. Beautiful, elegant in a simple dress of mossy green. "Hello, Rowan, I hope I'm not disturbing you."

The voice, that lilt of Irish hills. The eyes, warm, deep gold. "No, not at all. Please come in, Mrs. Donovan."

"I wasn't sure I'd be welcome." She stepped inside, smiled. "Since my son's made such a fool of himself."

"I'm glad to meet you. I'm sorry—I can't even offer you a chair."

"You're leaving then. Well, I'll give you this as a going away present." She held out a box of carved apple wood. "And as a thank-you for the drawing of Liam. They're chalks, the pastels you wanted."

"Thank you." Rowan took the box, grateful to have something to do with her hands. "I'm surprised you'd want to see me since Liam and I...since we argued."

"Ah." The woman waved a hand in dismissal and wandered the room. "I've argued with him enough myself to know it's impossible not to. He's a head like a brick. But his heart isn't hard."

When Rowan looked away, she sighed. "I don't mean to make you uncomfortable."

"It's all right." Rowan carried the box to the narrow counter that separated the living area from the kitchen. "He's your son and you love him."

"I do, very much. Flaws and all." She laid a gentle hand on Rowan's arm. "He's hurt you, and I'm sorry for it. Oh, I could box his ears for it," she snapped in a lightning change of mood that had Rowan smiling uncertainly.

"Have you ever?"

"Boxed his ears?" This time Arianna laughed, light and free. "Oh, with Liam what choice do you have? He was never an easy one. Girl, the stories I could tell you would curl your hair. Takes after his father, he does, and can go royal on you in a blink.

Now Finn would say it's my temper running through him, and he'd be right. But if a woman doesn't have spine and temper, men like that will march right over you."

She paused, studying Rowan's face and her own eyes filled abruptly with tears. "Oh, you love him still. I didn't want to look and offend you. But I can see it."

"It doesn't matter."

But before she could turn away, Arianna gripped her hands, gave them an impatient squeeze. "Love is all that matters, and you're smart enough to know it. I've come to you as a mother only, with no more than a mother's right, and a mother's heart. He suffers, Rowan."

"Mrs. Donovan—"

"Arianna. It's your decision to make, but you need to know. He's hurt as well, and missing you."

"He doesn't love me."

"If he didn't he wouldn't have made so many foolish mistakes. I know his heart, Rowan." She said it softly and with such simple faith, Rowan felt a flutter in her stomach. "It's yours if you'll have it. I don't say it because I want him to step into his father's place. Whoever he loved would have been welcome with joy. Don't turn your back on your own happiness just to hug your pride. One's cold without the other."

"You're asking me to go to him."

"I'm asking you to listen to your heart. Nothing more or less."

Rowan crossed her arms over her breasts, rubbed her own shoulders as she paced the bare room. "I still love him. I always will. Maybe part of me recognized him in that first instant. And my heart just fell at his feet.''

''And he didn't treasure it as he should have, because he was afraid of it.''

''He didn't trust me.''

''No, Rowan, he didn't trust himself.''

''If he loves me…'' Even the thought of it weakened her, so she shook her head, turned back with her eyes level, her hands steady. ''He'll have to say it. And he'll have to accept me on equal grounds. I'll take nothing less.''

Arianna's smile was slow, and it was sweet. ''Oh, you'll do Rowan Murray, for yourself and for him. Will you go back and see?''

''Yes.'' She let out the breath she hadn't known she was holding. ''Will you help me?''

The wolf raced through the woods, as if trying to outrun the night. The thin crescent of the moon offered little light, but his eyes were keen.

His heart was burdened.

He rarely sought sleep now, for the dreams would come no matter how he willed them away. They were always of her.

When he reached the cliffs, he threw back his head and called out for his mate. Even as the sound swept away the silence, he grieved for what he'd so carelessly lost.

He tried to blame her, and did. Often. Whatever form he took, his mind worked coolly, finding dozens of ways, small and large, to shift the burden to her.

She'd been too impulsive, too rash. She'd twisted his motives, his logic. Deliberately. She'd refused to see the clear-cut sense in everything he'd done.

But tonight that line of thinking did nothing to ease his heart. He turned away from the cliffs, outraged that he couldn't stop yearning for her. When the voice whispered, *love waits* in his head, he snarled viciously and blocked it out.

He prowled the shadows. He sniffed the air, snarled again. It was Rowan he scented, some trick of the mind, he thought, infuriated with his own weakness. She'd left him, and that was the end of it.

Then he saw the light, a gold glimmer through the trees. Tawny eyes narrowed as he moved toward the circle of stones. He stepped through them, saw her standing in the center. And went very still.

She wore a long dress the color of moondust that foamed around her ankles. Her hair was loose, flowing over her shoulders, with hints of silver shining in it from the jewels wound through. There was silver at her wrists as well, at her ears.

And on the bodice of her dress lay a pendant, an oval of moonstone in a setting of hammered silver.

She stood slim and straight behind the fire she'd made. Then she smiled at him.

"Waiting for me to scratch your ears, Liam?" She caught the quick flash of temper in his eyes, and only continued to smile.

The wolf stepped forward, became a man. "You left without a word."

"I thought we had plenty of words."

"Now you've come back."

''So it seems.'' She arched a brow with a studied coolness even as her stomach jumped with raw nerves. ''You're wearing your amulet. So you've decided.''

''Aye. I'll take my duty when it comes. And you wear yours.''

''My great-grandmother's legacy to me.'' Rowan closed her fingers around the stone, felt it calm her nerves. ''I've accepted it, and myself.''

His hands burned to touch her. He kept them lightly fisted at his side. ''I'll be going back to Ireland.''

''Really?'' She said it lightly, as if it meant nothing to her. ''I'm planning on leaving for Ireland myself in the morning. That's why I thought I should come back and finish this.''

''Ireland?'' His brows drew together. Who was this woman? was all he could think, so cool, so self-possessed.

''I want to see where I came from. It's a small country,'' she said with a careless shrug, ''but large enough for us to stay out of each other's way. If that's what you want.''

''I want you back.'' The words were out before he could stop them. He hissed out a curse, jammed his fisted hands into his pockets. So he'd said it, he thought, humbled himself with the words and the needs. And the hell with it. ''I want you back,'' he repeated.

''For what?''

''For—'' She baffled him. He dragged his hands free to rake them through his hair. ''For what do you think? I'll take my place in the family, and I want you with me."

"It's hardly that simple."

He started to speak, something ill-advised and much too heated he realized, and pulled himself back. Control might be shaky—*in the name of Finn, just look at her*—but it was still there. "All right, I hurt you. I'm sorry for it. It was never my intention, and I apologize."

"Well then, you're sorry. Let me just jump into your arms."

He blinked, deeply shocked at the biting tone. "What do you want me to say? I made a mistake— more than one. I don't like admitting it."

"You'll have to, straight out. You took your time deciding if I'd suit you—and your purposes. Once you decided what those purposes would be. When you didn't know about my bloodline you considered if you should take me and get out of the duty you weren't sure you wanted. And when you did know, then it was a matter of deciding if I'd suit you if you did accept it."

"It wasn't that black and white." He let out a breath, admitting that sometimes the gray areas didn't matter. "But yes, more or less. It would have been a big step either way."

"For me as well," she tossed back, eyes firing. "But how much did you consider that?"

She whirled away, and had him rushing after her before he'd realized he'd moved. "Don't go."

She hadn't intended to, just to pace off her temper,

but the quick desperation in the two words had her turning slowly.

"For pity's sake, Rowan, don't leave me again. Do you know what it was for me to come for you that morning and see you were gone. Just gone." He turned away, scrubbing his face over his hands as he struggled with the pain. "The house empty of you, and still full of you. I was going to go after you, right then and there, drag you back where I wanted you. Where I needed you."

"But you didn't."

"No." He turned to face her. "Because you were right. All the choices had been mine. This was yours and I had to live with it. I'm asking you now not to leave me again, not to make me live with it. You matter to me."

Everything inside her cried out to go to him. Instead she lifted her brows again. "Matter to you? Those are small words for such a big request."

"I care for you."

"I care for the puppy the little girl next door has. I'm not content with that from you. So if that's all—"

"I love you. Damn it, you know very well I love you." He snatched her hand to keep her from leaving. Both the gesture and the tone were anything but loverlike.

Somehow she kept her voice steady. "We've established I don't have the gift to see, so how do I know very well what you don't tell me?"

"I am telling you. Damn it, woman, can't you hear, either?" His control slipped enough to have sparks snapping in the air around them. "It's been you, all

along, right from the start of it. I told myself I
didn't—that I wouldn't until I decided. I made myself
believe it, but there was no one ever but you.''

The thrill of it—the words, the passion behind them
driven by as much anger as heart—spun through her
like rainbows. Even as she started to speak, he released her hand to prowl the circle much as the wolf
he favored.

''And I don't like it.'' He flung the words over his
shoulder at her. ''I'm not required to like it.''

''No.'' She wondered why she should feel delighted rather than insulted. And it came to her that
it gave her an unexpected, and desperately sweet
power over him. ''No, you're not. Neither am I.''

He whirled back, glaring at her. ''I was content in
my life as it was.''

''No, you weren't.'' The answer surprised both of
them. ''You were restless, dissatisfied and just a little
bored. And so was I.''

''You were unhappy. And the way you're thinking
now it's that I should have taken advantage of that.
Plucked you up straight away, told you things you
couldn't have been prepared to hear and carried you
off to Ireland. Well, I didn't and I won't be sorry for
that much. I couldn't. You think I deceived you, and
maybe I did.''

He shrugged now, a regal motion that made her
lips want to curve into a smile. ''You needed time,
and so did I. When I came to you as a wolf it was to
comfort. It was as a friend. And so I saw you naked—
and enjoyed it. Why shouldn't I?''

''Why indeed,'' she murmured.

"When I loved you in dreams, we both enjoyed it."

Since that was issued as a challenge, she merely inclined her head. "I don't think I ever said otherwise. But still, that choice was yours."

"Aye, it was, and I'd make it again if only to touch you with my mind. It's not easy for me to admit that I want you as I do. To tell you that I've suffered being without you. Or to ask you to forgive me for doing what I thought was right."

"You've yet to tell me what it is you expect from me now."

"I've been clear enough on it." Frustration shimmered around him. "Do you want me to beg?"

"Yes," she said after a very cool, very thoughtful moment.

His eyes went bright gold with shock, then dark with what she thought was temper. When he started toward her, her knees began to tremble. Then eyes narrowed, he was down on his.

"Then I will." He took her hands that had gone numb. "I'll beg for you, Rowan, if that's what it takes to have you."

"Liam—"

"If I'm to humble myself, at least let me get on with it," he snapped. "I don't think you were ordinary ever. Weak is something I don't believe you could be. What I see in you is a woman with a tender heart—too tender at times to think of herself. You're the woman I want. I've wanted before, but I've never needed. I need you. You're who I care for. I've cared before, but never loved. I love you. I'm asking that it be enough for you, Rowan.''

She'd been struck speechless, but found her voice as she laid a hand on his shoulder. ''Why did you never ask before?''

''Asking's not easy for me. If it's arrogance, that's how I am. Damn it, I'm asking you to take me as I am. You love me. I know you do.''

So much for begging, she thought and had to fight back a smile. He managed to look arrogant and not a little fierce even on his knees. ''I never said I didn't. Are you asking me for more?''

''For everything. I'm asking you to take me on— what I am and what I'll do. To be my wife, leave your home for mine and understand that it's forever. Forever, Rowan.'' The faintest of smiles touched his mouth. ''For wolves mate for life, and so do I. I'm asking you to share that life, to let me share yours. I'm asking you here, in the heart of this sacred place, to belong to me.''

He pressed his lips to her hands, held them there until she felt his words turn to feelings and the feelings rush through her like magic.

''I'll have no other but you,'' he murmured. ''You said to me that I held your heart in my hands, and that I'd never have another like it. I'm telling you now you have mine in yours, and I swear to you, Rowan, you'll never have another like it. No one will ever love you more. The choice is yours.''

She studied him, the way his face lifted to hers, how the light from the fire he'd taught her to make danced over it. She didn't need his thoughts to see now. All she wanted was there, in his eyes.

She made her choice, and lowered to her knees so their eyes were on level. "I'll take you on, Liam, as you'll take me. And I'll take nothing less than forever. I'll share the life we make together. I'll belong to you, as you belong to me. That's my choice, and my promise."

Swamped with emotion, he lowered his brow to hers. "God, I missed you. Every hour of every day. There's no magic without you. No heart in it."

He found her mouth with his, pulling her close, swaying as the force of feeling rocked him. She wrapped her arms around him, gave him every answer to every question.

"I could drown in you." He rose to his feet, lifting her high, and her laughter rang out pure and bright as she threw her arms up.

Starlight dazzled her eyes. She watched one shoot across the sky as he spun with her. A trail of gold, a shower of silver. "Tell me again!" she demanded. "Tell me now. Right now!"

"I love you. Now..." He lowered her until their mouths met again. "And ever."

She held him close, heartbeat to heartbeat. "Liam of Donovan." Leaning back, she smiled at him. Her prince, her witch. Her mate. "Will you grant me a boon?"

"Rowan of O'Meara, you have only to ask what you will."

"Take me to Ireland. Take me home."

Pleasure swirled into his eyes. "Now, *a ghra?*"
My love.

"In the morning." She drew him back to her. "It's
soon enough."

And when they kissed with the firelight glowing,
the stars shimmering, the faeries danced in the forest.
In the hills far away, pipes played in celebration, and
songs of joy were sung.

Love no longer waited, but found its mark.

* * * * *

Celebrate Silhouette's 20th
Anniversary with
#1 New York Times bestselling author

NORA ROBERTS

with the publication of Nora's very first
book, IRISH THOROUGHBRED, and
the exciting sequel, IRISH ROSE,
in this special 2-in-1 edition:
IRISH HEARTS

IRISH HEARTS will be on sale in
May 2000, at your favorite retail outlets.

Here's a sneak preview of the first story
in this wonderful duet,
IRISH THOROUGHBRED

The light of the half-moon guided Adelia as she strolled through the new smooth grass. The stillness, the familiar scent of animals, reminded her of home, and suddenly she felt a contentment and peace she had not even known she had lived without.

Hesitating outside the door of the large white stables, she debated whether she dare enter and spend the last of her evenings with the horses. Having decided there was no harm in it, she was reaching for the handle when an iron grip closed around her arm and whirled her around, and she was lifted off her feet for a moment like a rag doll.

"Just what do you think you're doing? And how did you get in here?"

She stared wordlessly at the owner of the harsh, angry voice, a vague shadow silhouetted in the dim moonlight, looming over her like an avenging giant. She searched for her own voice, but the combination of shock and pain had stolen it. Her words slipped down her throat and she felt herself being dragged into the building.

"Here, let's have a look at you," the voice growled as its owner switched on the lights. He spun her around, dislodging her cap, and the glory of her hair escaped its confinement to form a fiery cascade down her back.

"What the...you're a girl!" He released his firm hold and Adelia stepped back and began to give him both sides of her Irish tongue.

"Sure and it's observant you are to be noticing that—" She rubbed her arm vigorously while her green eyes glared up at her astonished assailant. "And who are you coming around grabbing innocent people and crushing their bones? A great, hulking bully you are, sneaking up on a body and dragging and pulling them about! A horsewhipping is what you're deserving for scaring the life from me and nearly breaking my arm in the process—"

"You may be pint-sized, but you're packed with dynamite," the man observed, obviously amused. "From your accent I could make a guess that you're little Dee, Paddy's niece."

"I'm Adelia Cunnane, but it's not your little Dee I am." She regarded him with open resentment. "And it's not me who's having the accent. It's you!"

He threw back his head and roared with laughter, increasing Adelia's fury. "Oh, I am glad to have made you so happy." Folding her arms across her chest, she tossed her head, rich dark curls swinging wildly. "And who in the world are you, I'd like to know?"

"I'm Travis," he answered, still grinning. "Travis Grant."

It was Adelia's turn to gape at her companion. As the mists of fury cleared from her eyes, she saw him clearly for the first time. He was tall and powerfully built, and the sleeves of his shirt were carelessly rolled above his elbows, revealing deeply tanned muscular arms. He had chiseled features, clear and sharp, and his eyes were so blue against the brown of his skin, that they startled the casual onlooker. His hair was rich and full, thick black curls in a disarming disarray to his collar, and the mouth that continued to grin at her was well-formed, showing strong white teeth.

This was the man she was to work for, this was the man she needed to impress, Adelia's brain registered numbly, and she had just raked him clean with a furious tongue. "Jakers," she whispered, shutting her eyes for a moment and wishing she could disappear in a puff of smoke.

"I'm sorry we met under such, uh..." he hesitated, his mouth twitching again—"confusing circumstances, Adelia. Paddy's been on top of the world since he made arrangements to bring you over from Ireland."

"I didn't expect to be meeting you till tomorrow, Mr. Grant."

"I didn't expect to find a half-pint fairy invading my stables," Travis returned, grinning once again.

Adelia straightened her spine and threw him a

haughty look. "I couldn't sleep, so I came for a walk. I was thinking I might look in on Majesty."

"Majesty's a very high-strung animal," Travis admonished, his gaze roaming over her from top to bottom. "You'd best keep a respectable distance."

"And how will I be doing that?" she demanded imperiously, disconcerted by his masculine appraisal. "I'm to be exercising him regularly."

"The devil you are!" His eyes rose to hers and narrowed. "If you think I'd let a slip of a thing like you on my prize colt, you've lost your senses."

"I've already been on your prize colt." Anger returned, her head tossed with it. "I rode around your track on him in fine time."

"I don't believe it. Paddy wouldn't let you up on Majesty."

"And I'm not in the habit of lying Mr. Grant," Adelia retorted with great dignity.

"You rode Majesty?"

"That I did," she agreed, then, noting the anger hardening the blue eyes, sped on. "He's a beauty, rides like the wind, but he's not bad-tempered. The poor thing just needed someone to show him he was loved and appreciated."

"And you can talk to horses?" Travis's lips curved on the question.

"Aye," she agreed, unaware of the mocking gleam in his eyes. "Anyone can if they've a mind to. I know animals, Mr. Grant. I worked with the vet back in Skibbereen, and I know a bit about healing as well. I would never do anything to bring harm to Majesty or any of your other horses."

He said nothing to this, only took his time studying her. As his silence and intense regard continued, she felt a small tingle of fear, mixed with another sensation, strange and foreign, that she was unable to decipher.

"Mr. Grant," she began, swallowing pride to plead. "Please, give me a chance—a fortnight, no more." She took a deep breath and moistened her lips. "If you don't want me after that, just tell me, and I'll abide by your wishes."

"All right, Adelia," he said at length. "You'll have your two-week trial, just between us."

A brilliant smile lit her face and she extended her hand. "Thank you, Mr. Grant. I'm grateful to you."

He accepted her hand, but his returning smile faded, a frown replacing it as he turned her palm up and examined it. Her hand was exquisitely small, fingers long and tapering, but it was rough and calloused from years of the abuse of labor. He raised his eyes and looked into hers. "It's a crime for such a tiny hand to be as hard and rough as any ditchdigger's."

Unaccountably stung by his softly spoken words, she jerked her hand away, holding it behind her back. "I'm sorry they're not as soft as a lily, Mr. Grant. But it's not a lady's hands I'll be needing for the job I'm doing for you. If you'll excuse me now. I'll be going in."

She moved past him quickly, and he watched her run like a rabbit across the grass and out of sight.

invites you to join the Brand brothers,
a close-knit Texas family in which each sibling
is eventually branded by love—and marriage!

MAGGIE SHAYNE

continues her intriguing series

with

THE OUTLAW BRIDE, IM #967

On sale December 1999

*If you missed the first five tales of
the irresistible Brand brothers:*

THE LITTLEST COWBOY, IM #716 $3.99 U.S./$4.50 CAN.
THE BADDEST VIRGIN IN TEXAS, IM #788 $3.99 U.S./$4.50 CAN.
BADLANDS BAD BOY, IM #809 $3.99 U.S./$4.50 CAN.
THE HUSBAND SHE COULDN'T REMEMBER, IM #854 $4.25 U.S./$4.75 CAN.
THE BADDEST BRIDE IN TEXAS, IM #907 $4.25 U.S./$4.75 CAN.

you can order them now.

To order, send the completed form, along with a check or money order for the total
above, payable to Heart of the West, to: **In the U.S.:** 3010 Walden Avenue, P.O. Box 9077,
Buffalo, NY 14269-9077; **In Canada:** P.O. Box 636, Fort Erie, Ontario, L2A 5X3.

Name: _____

Address: _____ City: _____

State/Prov.: _____ Zip/Postal Code: _____

Account # (if applicable): _____   075 CSAS

*New York residents remit applicable sales taxes.
  Canadian residents remit applicable GST and provincial taxes.

Visit us at www.romance.net   SIMTB

If you enjoyed what you just read,
then we've got an offer you can't resist!

Take 2 bestselling
love stories FREE!
Plus get a FREE surprise gift!

Clip this page and mail it to Silhouette Reader Service™

IN U.S.A.	**IN CANADA**
3010 Walden Ave.	P.O. Box 609
P.O. Box 1867	Fort Erie, Ontario
Buffalo, N.Y. 14240-1867	L2A 5X3

YES! Please send me 2 free Silhouette Intimate Moments® novels and my free surprise gift. Then send me 6 brand-new novels every month, which I will receive months before they're available in stores. In the U.S.A., bill me at the bargain price of $3.57 plus 25¢ delivery per book and applicable sales tax, if any*. In Canada, bill me at the bargain price of $3.96 plus 25¢ delivery per book and applicable taxes**. That's the complete price and a savings of over 10% off the cover prices—what a great deal! I understand that accepting the 2 free books and gift places me under no obligation ever to buy any books. I can always return a shipment and cancel at any time. Even if I never buy another book from Silhouette, the 2 free books and gift are mine to keep forever. So why not take us up on our invitation. You'll be glad you did!

245 SEN CNFF
345 SEN CNFG

Name _____ (PLEASE PRINT)

Address _____ Apt.# _____

City _____ State/Prov. _____ Zip/Postal Code _____

* Terms and prices subject to change without notice. Sales tax applicable in N.Y.
** Canadian residents will be charged applicable provincial taxes and GST.
  All orders subject to approval. Offer limited to one per household.
  ® are registered trademarks of Harlequin Enterprises Limited.

INMOM99   ©1998 Harlequin Enterprises Limited

Don't miss Silhouette's newest cross-line promotion,

Four royal sisters find their own Prince Charmings as they embark on separate journeys to find their missing brother, the Crown Prince!

The search begins in October 1999 and continues through February 2000:

On sale October 1999: **A ROYAL BABY ON THE WAY** by award-winning author **Susan Mallery** (Special Edition)

On sale November 1999: **UNDERCOVER PRINCESS** by bestselling author **Suzanne Brockmann** (Intimate Moments)

On sale December 1999: **THE PRINCESS'S WHITE KNIGHT** by popular author **Carla Cassidy** (Romance)

On sale January 2000: **THE PREGNANT PRINCESS** by rising star **Anne Marie Winston** (Desire)

On sale February 2000: **MAN...MERCENARY...MONARCH** by top-notch talent **Joan Elliott Pickart** (Special Edition)

ROYALLY WED
Only in—
SILHOUETTE BOOKS

Available at your favorite retail outlet.

Visit us at www.romance.net

SSERW

In November 1999 share in
the holiday magic as the
national bestseller that
captured readers' hearts is
now in paperback for the first
time—with an added bonus!

LONE STAR

Christmas...

AND OTHER GIFTS

Bestselling authors

DIANA PALMER
and
JOAN JOHNSTON

come together in one special Christmas collection
that brings readers four wonderful stories brimming
with dazzling romance and fiery passion.

Celebrate Christmas with four devastatingly
handsome heroes, including a most memorable
Long, Tall Texan and an infamous outlaw
from *Hawk's Way*.

A Christmas keepsake to treasure always!

Available at your favorite retail outlet.

Silhouette ®

Visit us at www.romance.net

PSLSC

Start celebrating Silhouette's 20th anniversary
with these 4 special titles by
New York Times bestselling authors

Fire and Rain
by Elizabeth Lowell

King of the Castle
by Heather Graham Pozzessere

State Secrets
by Linda Lael Miller

Paint Me Rainbows
by Fern Michaels

On sale in December 1999

Plus, a special free book offer inside each title!

Available at your favorite retail outlet

V *Silhouette* ®
™
Visit us at www.romance.net

PSNYT